The Longest Night Watch

Writers Colony Press

Published by Writers Colony Press
Print Edition
Cover designed by Sarah Anderson

Print Edition, License Notes

This book is dedicated to those who hold the longest night watch – the bedside vigil over those they love, and to whom they have become a stranger.

And to the memory of Sir Terry Pratchett - a man who held an impossible world in his mind and let us inhabit it for a time. GNU TERRY PRATCHETT.

The Longest Night Watch

All proceeds from this book go to support The Alzheimer's Association of America.

"Formed in 1980, the Alzheimer's Association advances research to end Alzheimer's and dementia while enhancing care for those living with the disease." – www.alz.org

Table of Contents

Foreword

Lacey Sutton, Editor

On the 12th of March, 2015, the world ended.

Alright, perhaps not *the* world, but *a* world - The Discworld – which had parallels (that were more like incisive perpendiculars) to our own. Which, over the course of some 63 books[1] and miscellaneous short stories, become refuge and inspiration to millions of readers. On that fateful date it slipped quietly into the night, along with its creator, Sir Terrence "Terry" Pratchett.

I cried when I learned the news. Sat sobbing away at my desk at work. I continued to cry for days as my heart broke with every fresh thought of loss and reminder of what would never be again. I was not the only one.

For many fans, March 12th did not mark the beginning of the grieving process for Sir Terry. That started December 11, 2007, when Sir Terry posted online about what would come to be known as his "embuggerance"- a rare form of Alzheimer's Disease which affected his back brain far more than the portions responsible for memory and language. It was a mixed curse – still ultimately fatal, it nevertheless allowed Sir Terry to continue writing (with assistance) until the day he died. When I saw him at a book talk in 2011 (not a book signing since he was unable to hold a pen for long periods of time by then), he was as clear, brilliant and hilarious as ever. He did not lose himself, did not lose his world, until our world lost him.

Most with Alzheimer's are not so "fortunate." Their memories, their identities, their sense of security with where they are and the people they are with, deteriorates much faster than their physical bodies. It is a slow, vicious killer. It attacks the core of the victim first. And unless caught in the

---

[1] And another 20 non-Discworld books   9

early stages, it leaves them with little opportunity to secure their legacy.

So it is to the topic of legacies that this anthology is devoted. As Sir Terry wrote in his book *Going Postal* - "A man is not dead while his name is still spoken."

In these pages, we have gathered a group of stories by authors who wished to carry on his tradition of humor, societal insight, and light-hearted entertainment. Our purpose was not to co-opt his characters and setting – these are not Discworld fan-fiction – but to honor the impact he made on our lives and our writing as best we can.

We also have authors who are carrying the flame of memory in honor of others lost to Alzheimer's. They have lived through the longest nights, holding the hands of beloved family members who could not remember their existence. The stories and poems they share are by their nature more poignant than humorous, and I hope the reader is as moved by them as I was.

Sir Terry and his Discworld will not truly be dead while those who found him an inspiration can pick up a pen. Every time one of Sir Terry's books is cracked open, light will return to the Discworld. But those of us here of the Longest Night Watch hope to not just keep our lanterns lit, but to spread their glow until no more of our loved ones are taken by the dark.

This anthology is part of a larger project in support of the Alzheimer's Association: The Longest Day. All proceeds from this book will be donated to the American Alzheimer's Association, and used in the fight against this terrible disease.

We hope this will become an annual event.

Our Authors

AKA, the Longest Night Watch

Andrew Barber is a novelist, poet and songwriter. Since beating  7,000 people to become the inaugural Poetry Rivals Slam Champion in 2010, he has completed three volumes of poetry and four books in the Cybermancer Chronicles. He has been a fan of Terry Pratchett's writing for most of his adult life.

Andrew contributed the poem "Death Played the Banjo" and the short story "Lords, Ladies and the Dracomorph", an excerpt from *Cybermancer IV: In The Midnight Hour*

Connie Cockrell began writing in response to a challenge from  her daughter in October 2011 and has been hooked ever since. Her books run the gamut from Sci-Fi to Contemporary stories. She's published two stand alone novels, a complete four book series and has now started a Dystopian Sci-Fi, a Cozy Mystery, and a Contemporary New Adult series along with three collections of short stories. She has been included in four different anthologies and published on Every Day Fiction. Connie continues to write about whatever comes into her head.

Connie Cockrell's participation in this anthology is especially poignant because not only has she loved each of Mr. Pratchett's works she's ever read, but her mother-in-law suffered from Alzheimer's.

If you'd like to know more, go to Connie's Blog or to her Facebook page.

Connie contributed the flash fiction story "Lying in Wait"

Joshua Cejka has been writing for roughly 35 of his 41 years and

loves every little last bit of it. Primarily focusing on mystery these days, he likes to stretch his legs occasionally, and is working on a series of books that combines the detective novel with fantasy.

Joshua Cejka is the author of the Meg Brown Mystery Series of books and the upcoming Stonemaiden's Cup. He lives in Wisconsin - for the moment - with his two cats, Dharma and Emma, and a desk full of effluvium which he occasionally must combat before it destroys him.

Joshua contributed the short stories "Out of Time" and "Cutlyn's Tale: The Crossroads"

Janet Gershen-Siegel is a freelance science fiction author and blogger for Boldly Reading, an online book club. Her latest project is a near-future detective trilogy, The Obolonk Murders. She lives in Boston with her husband and more computers than they need, and has watched helplessly as family members have been lost to Alzheimer's. You can visit her at http://janetgershen-siegel.com

Janet contributed the short-story "Props"

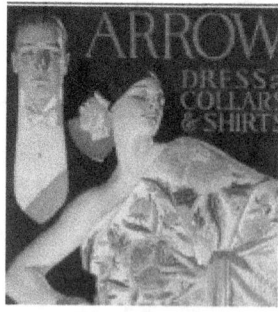

D.R. Perry has worked in direct patient care for a decade. She writes poetry and Historical Fiction in remembrance of her grandparents and clients. She lives in Rhode Island with her husband, daughter and their little dog too.

D.R. contributed the poem "Final"

When **Amanda Parker Adams** isn't playing with fabric, her computers, or tormenting her cats, she's expanding her universe with writing, photography and grad school. She's held a deep and abiding love for all things fantasy and science fiction as soon as she could hold a book right side up. Her maternal grandfather and mother both had Alzheimer's Disease. Her grandfather succumbed to cancer before his Alzheimer's progressed too far in 1990, but her mother died from end-stage Alzheimer's in 2013, a month shy of her 84th birthday. Her father was a WWII Veteran who passed away in 2014. Amanda learned to sew and cook from her mother, while her father taught her a lifelong love of photography and instilled the belief of never giving up on her dreams and passions. She resides in Portland, Oregon with her two cats, who both exasperate her and give her (mostly) unconditional love.

Amanda contributed the short story "Remember Me"

R.R Virdi is the author of *The Grave Report* series. He has worked as a mechanic, in retail, and now spends his weekends helping others build gaming PCs, all while continuing to write stories. An avid mythology buff, he keeps a journal following the fictional accounts of his character, Vincent Graves, and all the horrible monsters he comes across. He lives in Falls Church, Virginia, tinkering with cars, gaming computers, and chasing after his dog.

Ronnie contributed the short story "Chance Fortunes"

Michael Walton has never been able to pick a career field – he's torn between, "two-fisted paleontologist" and "international man of mystery." Writing passes the time (but alas, does not yet pay the bills) while he decides what he wants to be when he grows up. He has attended the Armadillocon writer's workshop and has made numerous contributions to the Orion's Arm Universe Project. Someday soon perhaps there will be a novel on the shelves with his byline on it, but for now he lurks in the shadows… waiting.

Michael contributed the short story "Blame it on Moonlight"

Lacey D. Sutton is a prolific writer and even more prolific editor. Meaning that this is the first piece of hers to be published, and not just subjected to endless rounds of revision. As a day job she wrestles with tSQL code, making data dance to her clients' whims, and her night job involves being at the beck and call of a small child and two giant cats. She is an annual attendee of the Sirens Women in Fantasy Conference, and a seven-time winner of the NaNoWriMo writing challenge. Alzheimer's claimed the lives of her maternal grandmother and two great-aunts, and although she never had much of a mind to begin with, Lacey uses writing as a way to download her brain before it's gone entirely.

Lacey contributed the short story "Bedtime Stories"

Death Played the Banjo
(For Terry Pratchett)

Andrew Barber

He taught me of headology,
Of Morris men, and why they dance,
Orang utans in libraries,
Elvish music, Vimes' romance.

Why the fairy wants the teeth,
And how the crown can wear the king.
He taught me something of belief.
He taught me bits of everything.

He taught me dwarves can still be tall,
How what we see is not enough.
Identity is cultural.
He showed the spircle in the rough.

He showed the jester on the throne
Who took the hippie for his wife.
He showed the maiden, mother, crone,
A Death that had a sense of life.

A vampire forsaking blood,
As everything is still a choice.
Well-fed wizards, clear as mud:
Truth speaks in a gentler voice.

My idols now are mostly dead:
I lost another yesterday.
Their bodies fade, but what they said
Will never lose its way.

The colour of magic can be seen:
It's on the spectrum in between
The hint of midnight on the sky
And Great A'Tuin's twinkling eye.

Lying in Wait

Connie Cockrell

"Look at that!"
"Oh my God, look how ugly that thing is."
"Is it real?"

I sigh inside my stasis field. It's the same thing day in and day out. If only we had crash landed in what they then called the Soviet Union instead of Roswell, New Mexico. My body would have been burned by now or dissected to molecules. This is just torture.

"No children, it's not real. This is a representation of what some people think aliens could look like."

Yeah, Teach. You just keep thinking that. The owners of this crappy museum know better but they like to keep the mystery. That's what keeps the yokels coming in. At night I can lower the field and stretch and get some water. Usually the janitor keeps a food bar and an alcohol called Jack Daniels in his locker in the back. Bless Xerion, or I'd have lost my mind decades ago.

One boy sniggered to his friend. "It's got no privates." They both giggled before the teacher rounded them up to look at the pictures of our crashed ship. Of course I have privates. How do they think we reproduce? Budding?

A small girl peered through the fingerprint smudges on my case. I can feel her brain working. This is a smart one. Maybe one of the ones we were sent here to contact.

"Anna, come over here and look at the ship pictures."

She peers closer--the electrons firing through her brain are giving off waves. You'd think the rest of the kids in the place would melt she's so intense. No, she eyes me once more then turns to rejoin her group. That's a relief. I've noted her brain pattern. Tonight I'll get on the wreck of a computer the owner has in his office and track her down. She's worth following.

I relax into the stasis and try to go to sleep. When the lights go out and the janitor is done, I'll get up. Since we crashed on Earth there has been a population explosion. One of these people will be the right one. Soon, I hope.

I want to go home.

Out of Time

Joshua L. Cejka

The 82nd Earl of Breadtown, 8th Duke of Duxburg, Lord Martin of Llamaville (known to those friends he pretended to have as Marty) was in a terrific hurry. In his wake, five scurrying attendants scribbled notes. Among the retinue there were two clerks, one professional hair designer, one heaving and gasping dialog coach, and a manicurist who'd been called at the last possible moment to attend to the Earl.

Those on the street, dawdling and unimportant as usual, watched the small mob scurry along past shops that slowly opened themselves in the hazy early morning sun like neglected ditchweed poppies. Those that watched their passage were either those caught accidentally still conscious in new sunlight or those to whom early morning consciousness was an unfortunate regular occurrence - a mistake of circumstance. Either way, both groups watched the zippy passage of the little band with a curious, languid attitude. It was a fine morning. Nobody but the band was in a hurry to push it along.

A cafe owner sluggishly brewed coffee at his little shop and watched them pass as he handed a Gigantor Double Espresso Mocha Lavender Double Mint to one of his regulars who'd recently shown up bleary eyed and moving exactly like a zombie might had it not slept in a very long time. Like lizards on a rock, they soaked in the heat from the fresh sun.

"What's with them?" the zombie customer said, one eyebrow hoisting itself slowly over his brow which still revealed the imprint of a discarded pillow. The cafe owner twisted a dial on his giant steam machine which took up all but the first five feet of his tiny, but luxurious cafe. He wasn't entirely sure what the dial was supposed to do but it always produced a nice satisfied whine and a brilliant plume of steam, which was exactly what he wanted in the morning.

The cafe owner looked up at the quickly receding mob with one still droopy eye.

"Dunno. Guess he's in a hurry."

"If he don't slow down, that dialog coach is gonna die."

The cafe owner shrugged.

"I see them every morning. Every morning it gets earlier and earlier and he's always in the same hurry. And every morning that Dialog coach looks like he's about to die. You'd think all the hurry would get him in shape, but nope. Want a biscotti?"

"What's a biscotti?"

"Sorta like a cookie but without the fun circular shape, drier, and it sucks all the moisture out of your face."

"Why would I want that?"

"They're a new popular thing. The newest. All the cool, educated people buy them now."

"No accounting for taste then."

"None whatsoever. You want one?"

"Might as well. Can't be thought of as a bumpkin, can I?"

The patron chomped into the biscotti, made a face like he'd just bit into an overworked dishrag, then nodded as he swallowed.

"Mmmm... Sophisticated taste."

"Right." The cafe owner nodded sagely. "Need today's paper?"

The patron grabbed what remained of his biscotti and the gigantor coffee.

"Might as well. Seems a good morning for taking it easy." He took the scroll from the Cafe owner and clamped it under his arm as he maneuvered around the steam pipes for the coffee machine that snaked out from the central device like a stationary mechanical octopus full of barely contained frothy fury.

"No executions today?" The cafe owner spun the dial on another knob, listening to the pleasant steam that came out in a wonderful single note. Once again, he pondered the knobs actual function besides producing pretty steam and single notes.

"No, Arfrd. Would you believe? All the executions have been put off today. Clean slate. I had five on the docket and the axe was nice and sharp. Not complaining though. Gives me time to review the upcoming client list." The executioner flapped open the paper, opening straight to the crime blotter page.

"I wonder what that's all about?"

"Dunno. You know bureaucracy, though. They only get their ducks in a row so they can panic them with a dog whistle."

"Do ducks even hear a dog whistle?"

"It's an idiom."

"You're an idiom."

"Just for that you don't get a tip."

Which, privately, was just fine for Arfrd. He always felt just a little unaccountably queasy at earning tips off of other peoples' necks.

Another customer, Darf, who was the clock tower's resident maintenance man slogged up to the counter. Darf and the Executioner[1] encountered each other every morning but never exchanged a word. Mainly, because Darf was on the clock[2]. Literally. He was responsible for making sure the bell tolled for who it was supposed to, when it was supposed to. Given the intimate relationship between their two professions, it was perhaps understandable that they habitually avoided each other's acquaintance over guilt that they shared.

---

[1] Whose actual name, no one knew. Even his mother had called him "The Executioner" since his exceptionally prolonged birth.

[2] And seeing as the clock in question actually floated above the city for most of the day, being 'on' it took on added meaning.

Darf drew a mocha which steamed and banged and chuffed away in the morning before producing a tinny whistle over their corner signifying its completion. He took the cup from the owner and sat at the little cafe table across from the Executioner.

"You have the sports pages?"

The Executioner lowered a corner of the paper and gazed at his unofficial coworker.

"Nothing wrong with the clock this morning?"

"Not a thing. Fit as a fiddle." Darf seemed a little flummoxed by it, as though he wasn't quite sure what he could do with himself without the urgent need to fix the bell. The Executioner pulled out the requested pages and handed them over, now a little flummoxed himself which he did not like. He'd become The Executioner mainly to avoid such sensations. There was enough confusion and disquiet in the simple act of becoming an adult that he'd long since chosen to avoid it in his employment choices. Executing was easy and there was always a nice and very sharp end to things. He liked it that way.

For a moment The Executioner shouldered a slight worry that they were actually about to have a conversation about all of those odd synchronicities that drove the two men together in such odd places throughout the years, but it appeared that the clock keeper was about as interested in that conversation as he was. He pulled the sports pages in front of his face to hide behind it.

"Not bad," the Clockkeeper muttered to the page while taking a sip of his coffee.

"What's that?" the Executioner said to his section as he flipped the page, reading about an incoming client who had had the misfortune of being born a troll and getting lost along the wrong street.

"Plenty of time to enjoy a morning. I could really get used to this. Oh dammit. The Duxburg Dragons got whalloped again."

"It's a rebuilding year,"[3] the Executioner said solemnly.

"Yep. Same as last year."

* * *

Elsewhere, The Earl scurried on and his retinue scurried along with him. He heard the huffing of the dialog coach over his shoulder, and though he worried a little about Diggy keeping up and staying alive, he simply didn't have time to worry too much.

"Time, Diggy?" he said over his shoulder.

"7:42, M'lud," Diggy the dialog coach heaved. The Earl considered breaking into a run, but for now the sprint walking was doing better and it was multitasking - getting his gluts worked on as he walked. The physical education tutors he'd had as a child, brutal though they were with their drooping uncaring eyes, dismissive sneer and horrible bullying, had told him that speed walking was much better than jogging.

He was grateful he'd had them all killed.

"Right then," the Earl heaved. "What time does the next train leave?"

"8 AM on the nose," Diggy returned, a slight wheeze dropped into his breathless heaving. It sounded like an elephant trying to blow up a leaking balloon with farts.

"On the Nose? Are you sure? Not on the Dot?"

Some papers rustled behind him. He heard a few of them scatter into the street as Diggy dropped some. He hoped they weren't important.

[3] The Duxburg Dragons have technically been in a rebuilding year since their inception 312 years ago. Spirits traditionally run high that this will, in fact, be 'their year'. Until the team actually takes the field and unceremoniously and collectively throws up on itself as they diminish themselves in the raw glare of expectations that - in doing so - they actually live up to.

"On the nose, m'lud," Diggy gasped. It was important to get these distinctions in the clear. He didn't want to be on the wrong platform leaving on the wrong train.

Not that that would ever happen. The Earl was very good with such things. He'd only put to death three or four assistants in the last three years for making him late. He hated to be late. The Nose platform was the first one in Nickel Station so that was even better. He instantly recalculated the time in his head. It gave him an extra fifty seconds so he slowed his pace to breakneck. Diggy gasped in relief.

Unfortunately, the rapid slowing of the pace meant that his hair designer nearly stabbed him in the skull with the hair pick she was trying to use on the curled knot at the back of his head.

"Ouch, Harry! Careful."

Harry, unbeknownst to her employer, rolled her eyes as she shifted her shoulder armor. She was used to stabbing things in the head. Her last job had been in Gladiation and before that Professional Adventuring.

"Sorry, m'lud."

He was beginning to think Harry hadn't much experience in the Hair Designing arena[4]. But she had some skill in creating the 'dashing careless actiony' look that was so much the rage these days[5]. He'd had his last hair dresser baked into Dragon Pudding for not keeping up with the times.

"Alright. Clerky 1. I need you to take a letter to the Marquis of Barknuckle." Another sound of rustling pages behind him and a louder sound of more spillage, this time of a few bottles of ink. The Earl didn't bother to look around. He was focused on a curious man leaning against the wall of

[4] Which was true, though she was very good in other arenas that usually involved screaming and very close, and sometimes not very close, shaves.

[5] She did this mostly by allowing nature and the Earls extremely rapid pace to take its course, and keeping out of the way.

a barber shop up ahead. The man appeared to be watching them. The closer they got the more he shoved away from the wall. This was not a promising sign. Too often these streets were choked with people who preyed on precious time with religious pamphlets, petitions, requests for mercy. They would rob whole milliseconds from you if you so much as made eye contact with their squalor.

"Dear Marquis. You are a snot. I will have your fifty bushels of bananas promptly by Thursday at... Clerky 2?" Clerky 2 was the official scheduler. Of all the positions in the Earl's retinue his was by far the most important and as such Clerky 2s had a very high turnover - as well as mortality - rate.

"The ships are moving for Angribad at 5 PM from Instantly Quay."

"Just say 5 pm, please Clerky 2. Be efficient."

"Aye, m'lud," Clerky 2 said like a man who'd swallowed a ghost pepper.

They were nearing the barber shop now, which was unaccountably busy though no one seemed to be in much of a hurry. A line of men sat in a circle of chairs outside, each one lazily reading papers and sipping coffee. Some were chatting, all were smoking. The curious little man had pushed the rest of the way off the wall and into their path.

"Excuse me, do you have a moment?" he said into the path of their collective inertia.

The Earl gave him a look, which should have done plenty to indicate the idiocy of the question, but it didn't. The Earl made a sharp turn at the corner, secure in the knowledge that his retinue would pay the little man as much attention as he just had. There were certain advantages to being an Earl and one of them was that you simply didn't have a moment for little men who looked like accountants and who stood around waiting for you outside of barbershops. I mean... barbershops after all. Who uses those? Civilized people had hair designers. The only thing barbershops were good for was quartets.

Besides, he was late.

Being late was the exclusive province and right of the upper class. Poor people were on time. The rich, as everyone knew, were fashionably late. They were expected to be. It was considered such bad form to be timely that prearranged parties were usually held entirely in individual quarters as the invitees raced to get prepared for an event no one showed up to. Tardiness was one of the only classes in Goldbastard University he managed to pass with flying colors. If one were to keep time in its proper station, it was important to cultivate a withering crop of disdain for it.

Up ahead he saw the massive purplish clock tower of the station hanging in the bright morning haze. The longer the day got the higher the enchanted tower clock floated above the city until at noon it was scraping the clouds before slowly descending again. When they discussed the idea in committee it seemed like a brilliant idea, and it was, for the most part, but since its enchantment there'd been more than a few complaints from citizens who fairly regularly stumbled into the great hole it made as it sank into the earth at night. It didn't help matters that the area around the station was a popular spot for taverns and, by order of the prostitution league, poorly lit.

As he watched, one of last night's unfortunates woke to find himself pinned to one of the towers spires, panicked, and rolled off, falling with a distant scream into the street.

"That reminds me, Clerky 1 - I need you to get some artichokes for this evening. I need them at the soiree by no later than... what say you Clerky 2?"

More papers spilled and a voice called out breathlessly from behind him.

"8 PM sir."

"Make it 7:45, please. You must make sure you shave some time, Clerky or these deliveries will be tardy. We can't have that now can we?"

Truth be told, Clerky 2 had already shaved an hour off of it, knowing the Earl's obsession with others punctuality. The event itself was scheduled to begin at 9, which meant it would be closer to 1 AM before anyone showed up, if at all.

They were still several blocks away. The Earl picked up his pace. He knew he would be early at this point but that meant nothing except a quick mental calculation to rejigger the temporal gears and set a different timetable. Being early was unforgivable and punishable by death as Clerky 2 versions A-G could testify to, if they could testify, which is difficult to do when six feet under poured concrete and missing tongues. Not that they would actually miss them, having no use for them anymore.

The haberdasher on Blump Street was just setting out his wares on the sidewalk as they approached. Seeing them coming, a prostitute who had been passing the time with the Haberdasher sashayed into the path. She naturally, and mostly accurately, had assumed that the Earl was about to proposition her and shook her head at him.

"Sorry, Marty. Hours are closed for today."

He tugged at a piece of newly stuck in place hair which his hair designer instantly rushed to fix with a disgusted huff he was philosophically impervious to hearing.

"It's alright, Roxanne. I'm late anyway," he said whistling by at as brisk a pace as he dared.

He was already well out of ear shot so he never heard her mutter "That would be a first," meaningfully to the haberdasher who dared a giggle.

He rounded a food cart and nearly ran into another fellow who looked almost exactly like the man who'd had the audacity to speak to him by the barber shop. The Earl risked a very rare double take, but even as the little man receded, the only way he could be certain it wasn't the same man was by distance and speed. He had the same dull eyes fixed on him from behind tortoiseshell spectacles, the same thinning hair, the same tweed jacket and dull cravat and was carrying the same things in his hands: a ledger and an abacus. But it couldn't have been.

That would have meant the man was actually moving faster than him and that was impossible unless he'd been running. He would have had to run past him.

"Excuse me, sir… Do you happen to have a moment?" the man's nasal voice dopplered[6] at him.

The man looked as though he were fetching something from the pages of the ledger, or about to read from it which was even worse. The Earl whipped his head back around and quickened his pace.

"Just a moment! That's all I require!" the man called out after him.

Not for the first time, The Earl considered the wisdom of hiring a Scoffer to add to his retinue, just for moments like this. It was so demeaning to have to do it himself, even inwardly as he now was. To think he had a moment that could be borrowed? Ha! Just the thought made his blood freeze and his heart skip a beat. And wasn't it just like little men like that? Give them a moment and they stole an hour. Well. He was not so wasteful with his time. The man would have to be quicker and much better armed to slow him down.

People didn't know it but it was very difficult for Earls to actively dislike someone. It meant you actually had to be around them and make enough of an impression for that impression to be decidedly negative. Earls avoided that sort of thing. It was best to keep peoples acquaintance to the period of time in which one could feasibly eat a bagel. Anything longer than that and you risked forming an opinion. Opinions of people were what Earls called relationships. If someone asked 'what is your opinion of so-and-so' it meant you actually had to have one. Which meant

---

[6] Freddy Doppler (1785 MA - 1542 MA), the greatest Ethermist accoustical engineer, theorized that the reason sound dispersed with distance was the increasing amount of etherdemons devouring it between a sounds origin and its recipient.

you had to spend time thinking about it. And that time could be much better spent elsewhere, like verbally abusing vague underlings thrown in your path or getting in a (very) quick little fun with a woman of the night, or advising rulers about which laws for the protection and prosperity of the average citizen they ought to relax for the sake of making the uber-wealthy even uber-wealthier.

Dislike rising to the level of Hate… well that was unheard of. Earls were rich enough that Hate was a commodity they didn't have to afford.

"Harry? Did you see that?" He tried to transfer his scoffing to her, as she seemed the most capable of bearing it.

"See what, sir?" Harry was still working on his hair. She hadn't seen anything. "Umm, sir?"

Her eyes connected with his for a second, and then drifted to the direction her hairpick was pointing. He whipped his head back around and realized he was about to collide with another cart, this one with a fire under it to warm the brine in which morning sausages were broiling.

"Sausage, sir?" The vendor held one out for him but at his speed all he could do was try to wear it as a tie for which it was not designed. A clatter of coins on the street behind him spoke of Clerky 2's efficiency.

The Earl cursed. Behind him Clerky 2 made some adjustments to the Earls timetable on the paperwork that rapidly receded behind him in a flurry. Now they really were going to be late.

The Station loomed on their left. It was a massive building that looked as though it had been carved out of coal by an architect for the byzantine and diabolical. Looking at it, you got the impression you might see a long train car leaving it yanked along the rail by a very old and very ornery dragon. It was full of pointy bits like a hedgehog that had been singed, petrified, and grown into a monstrosity that belched out trains.

The Earl loved it. It was his favorite place on earth. He loved the rapidly switching timetables on the wall clicking over like a waterfall of time. He loved the sound peoples feet made on the obsidian tiles. He loved the low burble of sound in the great empty space, like a river of people all more or less on time. He loved the way the black polished stone refused to soak up the light from the oil lanterns scattered throughout. Even with the remains of a sausage for a cravat, he felt his heart skip a beat with glee.

He made the turn on Seamstress Street and waited as patiently as he could for a hole to appear in the dusty haze of the cart and carriage traffic in front of him. One of his clerks behind him careened off of another of his clerks at the sudden stop.

A weapons cart going somewhere with a load of bombs passed lazily by, the horse looking bored and blissfully unaware of the thousands of pounds of death behind him. It was the perfect opportunity. The purple velveteen carriage behind it was at what it inaccurately presumed was a safe distance. He jumped into traffic and was about to thread the needle between the bombs and the carriage when he was nearly dashed to pieces by a rickshaw toting the same little man with his abacus. He saw the little man wave the ledger in the air much like he would have had it been a religious pamphlet.

The Earl dodged like one of the Duxburg Dragons tripping over his own feet. He heard the now familiar refrain.

"Excuse me, sir? Do you have a moment?"

"No!" he threw behind him as he launched himself into the throng feeding themselves through the great brass door at the station entrance. The mob of big hats, shawls and coats swallowed him before he could get his head back around. That was all right. He'd had more than enough of that little man.

The dusty clatter of the street subsided inside the station and it opened up into that heavenly vacuous din - the burbling of the masses - like ocean waves on a relatively calm day. His feet clacked against the tile. He was home. The timetable clicked over, seemingly just for him and it cascaded an updated list of arrivals. A Mage and his coterie of well-behaved creatures cocked a bushy eyebrow at him as he zipped past to the ticket counter.

"Seven tickets for the Earl, please. On the 8:55 to Branigan?" He gave the ticket girl his best fetching smile. He even loved her little purple pillbox hat. He was home. In a different life he should have owned and operated a station like this. He pictured himself in the role, hovering over arrivals and departures, eking out maximum efficiency, swept into a dream of schedules with the chuffing noise of train wheels sluggishly keeping time with his dreams.

To him, the common rabble vanished in the persona of the station workers. In his mind they were interwoven with the work of trains, comings and goings. In reality, they might be bums on the street to whom he didn't even owe the tiniest bit of dignity, but here they were trainsmen. Shining gods doing battle with the ebb and flow of the universe.

She looked at the sausage stain on his chest as though it had just requested the tickets.

"I'm sorry, sir, the 8:55 has been delayed."

The words broke like wind on him, as though he'd stood too close to his bilious dialog coach after a meal of beans and elk. He applied a corresponding expression to the words and, by extension, the ticket seller's face but she was far too accustomed to disgusted, angered, or impatient travelers to even notice. It was another reason he loved the place. Even the common disdain that his class flung at them on a regular basis became dull over time. They ate mortal threats on their lives for breakfast and spit them out. If there was a superior being in the universe, he figured it had to be a train-man.

"Are you sure? Can't you check again?"

The demon who lived in the ticket sellers box popped the lid and stood angrily on the top.

"She's sure, bub. What, you think you're the only one going to be late today?"

"Surely, there's another train?" he said pleasantly at the demon who stood with its tiny hands on its tiny red hips.

"Oh righto, Mr. Big Pants. I must have forgotten all about the OTHER train. Oh. Right. Just a sec. Wendy, print him a ticket for the OTHER train."

For a moment, the Earl was elated as the demon flung himself back into the hatch in the top of the box. There was a grinding noise and the sound of scribbling as a ticket flipped through the slot in the counter. He felt great. Until he looked at it.

"ONE Ticket to 'CHILLYOURCHEEKSVILLE' - Have a seat bub," it read.

He took the ticket and turned to the sound of tiny sinister snickering coming from inside the box.

His retinue looked worried. their eyes bounced off of one another's like a caffeinated rubber ball in a raquetball court. They all knew the score: being late was the one thing the Earl could only be on his own choosing. Well, their second gaze bounced back, it's not like it's the ONLY thing you could lose your head for. No. That's true, said the third and fourth glances. But it is the quickest way.

"Well..." the Earl interjected among all the glances. "You might as well all have a seat."

He sounded cheerful but it was the sort of cheer that was sodden with depressed reflection, like a man trying to make the best of the corpse of his favorite parakeet by contemplating some sage seasoning and a marinade.

The tendrils of tension that bound them together in a mess of frayed nerves snapped and they all took a step back in unison, unsure of what to do with themselves and waiting for the other boot to drop - probably on one of their faces. If one were to see all of the nerves and the electrical current that bonded them together one would have seen it like a wet hairball upon which some rain had just fallen. They collectively did as they were bidden: relaxed into the most frightened semblance of repose they thought they could get away with.

The Earl didn't bother to look. Time slowed. All the figures of the well dressed travelers who, just moments ago, had been part of the blurry backdrop of his triumph were now watchful extras in his tragedy. A woman with what appeared to be an ornery cat on her head met his gaze and then looked away as she lifted a suitcase. A young boy with his finger diligently exploring the mysterious cavern of his nose smiled at him as though he'd just discovered an artifact there. A man, allegedly accompanying the other two, let his gaze linger on the posterior of a passing female train attendant. The Earl saw all of these things as though for the first time. He'd never needed to look beyond the whizzing blur of the world before and if this was the world of regular folk, he thought, you could just ram it. It was unnerving. It was unsettling. It horrified him to think that there was actually icky messy life wandering around doing things that had nothing to do with him.

Of course the man would be there. The one with the abacus. He spotted him across the great open expanse of the waiting gallery. For a moment he felt like he could hear the man's echoing footfalls above all the others. And then he was quite sure of it. Because time slowed again. Distant clacking steps became one long clack reminiscent of an auditory fly smacked against a window and then streaked by an aural flyswatter. People's motions blurred as though someone with a big wet napkin were trying to clean them off with a little solution.

The man with the abacus kept coming. The smile on his face was kind and patient, like the smile on an auditor upon being presented with a single crumpled and soggy receipt as proof of expenses.

He looked to his retinue. Their faces were caught glancing at each other, stuck in a shared moment of frozen panic.

The closer the man with the abacus got, the more time slowed. It was as if he were sucking all of it out of the room, which - in fact - he was. By the time he presented himself in front of the Earl with a resounding clack of his rather sensible professional shoes, you could have heard a pin fail to drop in the background caesura of stolen noise.

The father's eyes never left the bum of the stewardess person. The kid's finger made camp inside his nose. The woman with the cat on her head looked off forever over his right shoulder. He could move into her field of vision but it wouldn't be the same. She would never be looking at him.

"Hello," the man with the abacus said crisply in the crisp air. "Would you happen to have a moment?"

The Earl goggled at him. Goggling idiotically is apparently the perfect expression when one is faced with someone who could not only dance between the raindrops but carry on the longest waltz in history between them.

"Well…" he tried, wondering if his voice was going to work. "Yes. I rather think I have."

"Good." The man clicked something on his abacus and marked it in his ledger. "May I have it back then?"

"Excuse me?"

The little man shifted the abacus a little and licked his thumb while paging through the ledger.

"Well… it seems you have been the recipient of 8396 individual units of time on credit, and that you have actually pilfered increments of time on 25 different occasions. Consequently, I would ask that if you have a moment to spare, you give it back immediately."

The Earl was conscious of the fact that his dropped jaw was drawing much more air than usual, but he'd apparently lost control over it so it simply hung open.

"And if I don't?" he ventured once he'd finally rediscovered the slack muscles. It wasn't that the Earl was feeling terribly clear on what the little man was saying, it was simply a default answer to any question delivered by such little men. Inwardly, his brain tripped over itself and landed on its face.

"Well...it is standard audit procedure in these situations to request the increments back, if that is considered not forthcoming or if you show signs of evasion my protocol dictates that I escalate collection to a higher authority."

"Which is what again?"

The accountant smiled. It was the sort of smile a tiger might give to a still kicking antelope haunch - full of sympathy and understanding and very sharp teeth.

"Well... we have several options at that point. It all depends on the level of the infraction and the extent of the evasion."

"Could you give me a hint?"

"Well... you know when you refuse to pay a bill and people call you incessantly at all hours of the day?"

"Yesssss?" Even with all of his money and budgeteers who paid his bills, he sometimes refused to pay them out of principle. The principle being that he was important and important people, in order to continue being considered important, had to carry some bits of debt around with them or be considered phonies. It was similar to the idea of the Coal Adjutant making 80,000 pounds a day and still taking out a loan to buy a shack in the woods for 80 pounds that he would never live in or even visit but could also make sure no one else lived in either. Sure, you COULD buy it outright, but you wanted the Money Mages to augur your worth better. Divination like that had to have something to work with. And everyone knew that TRUE poverty was the exclusive province and plaything of the very rich. Only they could claim it openly. The poor could only be embarrassed by it and try vainly to escape it.

"Well..." the auditor continued. "It's a bit like that. Only more intrusive. And unpleasant."

"I seriously doubt it could be more unpleasant than bill collectors," he scoffed.

"You might be surprised."

"Surprise me." The Earl was feeling feisty even though there was a little bit of his spleen that was screaming for him to stop. "You can actually be more annoying than calling me at dinner or during my favorite puppet show? Can you use a terrible foreign accent as well?"

"Well... yes. Of course. We wouldn't be who we are if that was our only recourse."

"And exactly who are you?"

The little man flicked a business card out of a little pocket on the ledger. The Earl read it. It read 'Time' and that was all.

"I thought... but you don't look like..."

"What exactly were you expecting me to look like?"

"Well... to be honest I always pictured you as an old man with a diaper."

"You're thinking Year. He's one of my employees actually. Lazy bastard. Does nothing but show up and get drunk at New Years parties. I suppose that's what we pay him for. If we paid him. Which we don't of course. You can't exactly pay a year with more time now can you? Ha ha. How would that look?" The accountant seemed to think that was very funny. It was telling that Time's jokes were about as amusing as a tax auditors[7] would be.

"We do, however, dock his pay once every four years. It was all due to that one in 1455. He stepped way out of line

[7] The 'jokes' segment of the tax auditors convention of 1765 had a record number of suicides - 45. At first the constables had assumed the Sisters of Deeply Profound Compassion had snuck in and executed them, until closer examination. One of the auditors had swallowed his own tongue. On purpose.

and tried to put the moves on Second. Can't have that. Very unprofessional."

"I still don't understand what any of this has to do with me?"

"You are out of time."

"Excuse me? Do you mean I'm dying?"

The accountant smiled his little smile. Somehow, the Earl got the feeling that Death's grin would be much friendlier.

"No. Though…" He could just see the accountant's dark eyes above the rim of his glasses. "We are on quite good terms, for the most part. He is on speed crow[8]. " The accountant pulled his coat lapel aside so that the Earl could just see the red eyes of the messenger crow resting in a jacket pocket.

"No," he continued. "You have been living on borrowed time. And your line of credit has come due. According to our records you owe The Temporal Authority 8000 units…"

"Plus interest?" The Earl ventured around the lump in his throat.

"No. We are not usurious bandits. Besides, as far as I understand the current economics of Time Management, there is no way to charge interest. Though it is an interesting idea, don't you think? I suppose we could do as we usually do but allow time to run backward for a time… I suppose that would really get their attention wouldn't it?"

With a little horror at what fresh hell he'd wrought, the Earl watched as the accountant jotted down a note in the margins of the ledger. He appeared very satisfied with it.

"Now then. How do you intend to pay? We take payments in moments, minutes, seconds…"

The Earl's thoughts dashed around in his head as though being chased by a tiger in spectacles.

---

[8] It is well know that the divine entities of the ether communicated by messenger crow.

"Give me a moment...," he said, trying to stall for time. It didn't work, of course because he was standing right there.

"I'm sorry. I thought I explained that is exactly the problem. Give *me* a moment. In fact, you must give me 8000 of them."

"Just a second...," the Earl tried again.

"No sir. We cannot extend any more credit."

"Okay. Fine. So you want it right this instant."

"Instant is good, yes. 8000 instances is better."

"So how, exactly, do I pay back time?"

"Well, you have to give it of course. I thought that was clear. We take it in moments, minutes, and seconds. Well... not WE, technically. Time, of course, has no use for time. We have quite a lot of it, in fact. You must give it to those who have little of it."

The Earl thought about that for a moment. He thought he was getting the hang of it insofar as there was a distinct tightening feeling around his neck that was decidedly less than pleasant. He would have to give time. That meant, as far as he was able to figure, he would actually have to listen to people who pestered him with all the things that sociable, well-to-do people were generally exempt from. He would have to be temperate, sanguine, hospitable. It was really quite unfair, and if you know wealthy people you will know that fairness is something they know quite a bit about. They are masters of fairness, insofar as that fairness applies to them at the expense of others. Anything that could be considered fair for everyone quite obviously wasn't fair to them because they, naturally, had special circumstances one should consider. It wasn't fair that people didn't properly see wealth and privilege for the burden it clearly was. This deficit of justice alone was enough for them to carry a well-honed grudge at the injustice meted out upon them by the entire human race. Correcting this injustice was the duty and honor of everyone of his particular stature.

"I won't do it. You can't make me."

Time stopped.
Time grinned.
Time nodded.

Then, Time snapped his fingers. The earl knew that snap. It was the same one he thought he'd invented when the Soupmaker brought his bisque in twenty seconds too late for it to be the appropriate temperature. It was also eerily reminiscent of what happened to the Soupmakers neck.

A giant man whose eyes had been swallowed by a considerable forehead and then covered over with a mountain of a brow walked into view in an impeccable coat. The earl noted the mountain of his brow had volcanoes in it but they might have been his eyes.

"This is one of my associates. You may call him Hour. Hour, this is Lord Martin."

"Absolutely charmed, sir." A cavern opened in the man's mouth. It was in the shape of a bright smile, but the smile stopped well short of getting singed by the volcanoes in his brow. Hours teeth were very white in that way that makes you immediately imagine them covered with blood.

"I can take violence," the Earl said bravely, though he had never actually tried. He was an earl. It was just understood in the context of the injustice of his privilege that certain violences might be visited upon him by those who did not appreciate or acquiesce to the rather weighty position he held on the scales of justice.

"Oh no. Hour is not a violent man. At least not in the context you understand. Hour...?"

Hour gently placed his hands on the Earl's sloped shoulders. It was gentle in that it felt only like two great rocks landed on him. The Earl stared at his teeth. He could see himself in them, which was very unnerving over the layer of imagined blood. There was a swift movement. Then there was a pain which the Earl decidedly could not take. He would like to give it back. Quickly. Unfortunately, that might have entailed reaching up through his own bum to retrieve the privates that had somehow just lodged themselves in his sternum.

That was only where the horror started. The Earl tried desperately to get his hands down to cover what was left of his nethers but they were stuck. In fact, everything seemed stuck. He couldn't move his eyes. Even sweat, which should have been pouring down his face in waterfalls, refused to come. There was only the pain. Raw, fiery pain that scorched and seared every last bit of earldom and manliness out of him. Unending horrible pain. And he was stuck with it.

Time played out before him in that he was smiling and doing a little dance.

"Sorry about that. Unpleasant business Time collection."

Oh dear god. Kill me now, the Earl tried to say. But of course his lips didn't move and his throat refused to make any noise, even the choking sob that it desperately needed to. He wasn't even breathing. No cool refreshing air came through his teeth. But he wasn't suffocating either and the metronome of his heart - which should have been thudding out like a woodpecker with a espresso addiction - had somehow stopped.

"We want to show you the consequences, you see. All the time you've stolen from others, all the borrowed time. This is the unpleasant reaction, you see? It's a simple transaction. Now, then. You have an Hour. He will be here with you. I think, at the end of it, you will see HOUR side of things. Get it? Hour? Haha."

The pain didn't end. The moment lingered. He stayed there staring at the frozen world. His eyes didn't water. Time left him both literally and figuratively. An hour passed before him. Repeatedly in fact. He wandered through the great hall, his heavy footfalls echoing throughout the room. The Earl heard him tap dance once and was surprised to consider that he was quite good at it, but the pain didn't disperse. It stayed with him, just as strong trapped within him and playing with his perfectly normal working mind like a giant dumb bully playing with a wheezy asthmatic kid in glasses.

Then, just as suddenly as the pain roared through him, it stopped. The world spun on. Feet that had been suspended in mid step finally touched ground, voices trapped mid consonant finally found a vowel. But it wasn't the same. Or not quite the same. He was still in the train station but it was as though someone had poorly spliced a new reality onto the old one. The light was slightly different. New people suddenly winked into the world mid-step replacing others who winked out of it.

His Hour was up. He would never get it back and that was quite a good thing as far as he was concerned. He'd never see another hour quite like it, but would always remember that hour for the rest of his time. It made quite an impression which was confirmed by his physician the next day when he went to see him.

He let out a breath and watched it go into the room, thankful that he had it to give. He took another breath to make sure the first one wasn't a fluke.

"You alright, boss?" Harry the Hair Designer looked up at him. He'd never really looked at her before. He'd simply told his man he'd needed a hair designer, not even knowing what one was. The rich were like that. If a rich person had something it immediately elevated it to the level of a need in the mind of the others. He still wasn't certain what there was to hair that required it be designed.

"Harry!" He smiled, enjoying the sublime pleasure of being able to sit beside her on the bench. "Let me ask you a question, if I may…"

"Yessir?" she said hesitantly. He wasn't sure what a hair designer was supposed to look like but he was pretty certain they weren't supposed to look as though they could crush nuts between two extremely muscular fingers. And he couldn't imagine why she insisted on wearing armor.

"How did you come to be in my service?" He was feeling decidedly sanguine about it now. Magnanimous. That was something else the rich could afford to be that others could not.

"Well... got hired through the adventurer service, m'lud."

"Adventurers? Interesting. Tell me more."

"Yes, M'lud." She hesitated, testing it to see if it was a trap. "But I'm sure you don't want to hear about it, sir. It's a bit of a long story, really. I don't want to bore you..."

He looked across the room. Standing under one of the great ornate windows was a little man in glasses. It looked, from the distance, that he was carrying an abacus in one hand. The Earl shuddered.

"I have nothing but my time to give," he said. As if on cue, a crew of bald men in orange bedsheets appeared dancing to the tune of a tambourine, which of course has no actual tune and the dancing reflected that.

"Excuse me, would you have a moment to hear about our lord and master the deity Gorgonzola?"

The Earl sighed.

"Yes. Of course. I have 7,999 of them in fact," He said. This was going to be a very long year.

Props

Janet Gershen-Siegel

Day 18. I think.

I've been here for a while. They pulled me out of my home and took me. And now I'm away from my son and all the old familiar things. There's too much that's unfamiliar, but that's to be expected, because the people keeping me aren't human.

I'm not really sure what kind of a place this is, but when the aliens got me here, they just kind of dumped me with not so much as a bye your leave. And so I'm here, but God only knows where here truly is! It's odd, like an approximation of an apartment but there's only one room. Well, a bathroom, I suppose, though the mirror doesn't seem to work right. Otherwise, it's just a bedroom with a pair of twin beds. And that's all it is. There are minor decorations on the wall - including a large crucifix - I guess the aliens don't understand what Jews are. The walls are a dull off-white, kind of an eggshell color. The bedding's predominant color is - ugh - pink. The closet and dresser are tiny and, if the second bed is any kind of an indicator, I'm supposed to be sharing both with someone else. But I guess the aliens don't realize that I am a woman and I like having a change of clothes and some makeup and all of that.

Day 26

The thing about these aliens is; everything is slightly ... off. They don't seem to understand, for example, the concept of fashion. They mainly wear uniforms, meant to look like, I think, doctors' scrubs. They've all got nametags, too, in order to bolster the illusion. They come in and introduce themselves but their names are meaningless because they came from TV broadcasts and movies and whatever we are broadcasting out to the sonic ether. Whether they are hearing soap operas or the news or some ham radio operator or a video blogger, well, they're not telling.

Day 35

They can't seem to get the look of us humans quite right. Every single subject looks old and careworn. Even a child I saw, a little girl – she looked careworn. If I were an alien and had a human test subject, I tell you, I would get this right. But their lack of quality control tells me that there are opportunities if I keep a look out for them.

Day 39

They presented me with a roommate. It was another approximation of a human; I like to call them props. They're all props in this alien movie where they're investigating and trying to understand my mind. So the prop roommate is named Margie. She barely speaks and farts and snores and is otherwise unremarkable.

Day 42

It looked like it was snowing outside, so I went outside. And it was as cold as a mother! So if they were faking the snow - if it was prop snow, that is - well at least the aliens knew enough to make it freezing cold outside. Then they got me indoors. It was warmer, so I thank them for that, but they scolded me and told me that I can't go outside without someone being with me. I didn't tell them, of course, but I'm looking for ways to escape. As for what I'll do after I leave this facility or holding center or prison or laboratory or whatever they're calling it, well, I have no idea. But alien societies always have rockets parked somewhere or other, or resistance cells. I'll figure it out as I go.

Day 51

There was singing or at least it sounded a little like singing and I asked why and one of the alien prop people told me it was Christmas. But if it really is, then it's another alien approximation. There's a tree and ornaments but the tree is fake. We got turkey to eat and it was dry.

Day 67. I think

There were two pink paper hearts taped to the door today. One had my name on it - spelled wrong. Stupid aliens. The other had Margie's name on it. Somebody said it was Valentines' Day. One of the old man prop people kissed my cheek and then groped me. I hauled off and whacked him in the face. Then the prop people brought me back to the room. I don't care. The whole thing is so annoying. Plus I already had cake. It was too sweet and it was dry.

Day 70

I was woken up really early. It was all lights and noise and prop people going in and out of the room. Then they brought in a bed with wheels and took prop alien Margie out and I got some sleep, finally.

Day 72

The props told me that Margie was dead and they were kind of surprised – in their approximate, alien, prop, not-quite-right kind of way – that I didn't feel bad. Well I don't. Who cares about props? They said they'd make me an appointment.

Day 76

I went outside again. It was warmer than last time, but still pretty damned cold. The walkway is all uneven and rough – I noticed this because I was barefoot. But you see, you never know when you get a chance to make a break for it. So I went outside even though I had no shoes on. Plus I wanted to see how long it would take them to figure it out, and how far I could get. They scolded me but I didn't pay attention, and then they mentioned an appointment again.

Day 83

I had the appointment. It was a prop room all done up with doctor props. You know, a prop diploma from some school I never heard of, a prop examining table, prop tongue sticks, all of that. The doctor was this short, fat, balding guy. He asked me a bunch of questions. Now, since he's an alien and I'm no fifth columnist, I didn't give too many straight answers. He asked my name. So dumb! I know he's got the file, so I gave it. But then he asked for year of birth and I said 1947. It's my favorite fake year. See, I was really born in 1962, so 1947 is a joke. He also asked what year it was and I guessed 2047. He told me not to go outside anymore without anyone being with me.

Day 91

They brought this new prop in. The prop was done up like a young woman and she said her name was Emily. I told her that I was onto them and their props. She took some notes. She said she's the social worker for my case — whatever that means. Those aliens keep getting better with their deceptions. But I keep figuring them out.

Day 100

Emily came back and asked me if my family had visited me during Christmas and I said no because you know Earth is pretty far away. She then took me outside and we walked around a little bit. It was warmer, which is good.

Day? I don't know what day so I'll start renumbering.

Day 1

There was more singing and another kiss and grope and so I slapped someone silly. They didn't like that and so the props called Emily I think and told her what I did.

Day 4

Emily came back and told me she found my boy. She showed me a picture on some little device. I didn't recognize the man in the picture. She told me he was not a little boy but I know my son is a small child. So that makes no sense. Emily said the singing the other day was for my birthday. But that makes no sense, either. I haven't been here for more than a few weeks. I think.

Day 6

The props are back. Emily came back with the man in the picture. The face is a little close to my boy but not really. They took me into the bathroom but the mirror doesn't work right. It's all just props.

Day 8

I went outside again. This time I got mad when they brought me back in and I hit a few people. Maybe Emily. Maybe the props. I was taken to the prop doctor office again. He asked me the year and I said 1947 and then he asked when I was born and I said 1947 and he asked how old that made me and I said if he was so smart he could do the math hisself.

Day 9. I think

The door is locked. There's no slot for a tray so I'm gonna starve in here.

Day 9. Still

They let me out for food. It's really bland. I don't know what kind it is.

Day?

It's later. I'm cold and my arm hurts.

Day?

My arm hurts.

Day?

Prop doctor has me in prop hospital. Said I had a heart attack.

Day?

Pretty girl came to see me. Said she's named Emily. Brought some guy with her. He looks a little like my boy.

Day?

Cold. Shakes all over.

Day? Cold

Coroner's Report on Death of Sarah Nichols

April 14, 2050

Subject reportedly died today and was found by the overnight nurse.

Autopsy waived by son, as his mother apparently suffered from Alzheimer's disease. Explained to closest living relative that an autopsy is the only way to truly be certain, and it is of some help with scientific research into cause and cure.

The deceased's son still refused an autopsy. Signature was obtained and is on file.

Cause of death of this 87-year-old Caucasian female appears to be either a Cardiovascular Accident [CVA] or Myocardial Infarction; either would be complicated by Alzheimer's. Body does not appear to have suffered any exterior physical trauma.

Body has been transferred to the Feldman-Shapiro Funeral Home for cremation.

Cause of Death: Cardiovascular Accident CVA or Myocardial Infarction, complicated by Alzheimer's syndrome.

Copy to Emily Chen, Social Worker.

Lords, Ladies and the Dracomorph

Exert from *Cybermancer IV: In The Midnight Hour*

Andrew Barber

Debbie had no idea where she was, although she at least knew she was still trapped within the videogame that had been her prison for as long as she could remember.

She'd selected the role playing game they'd played before, trying to find somewhere she felt at home, somewhere she would fit. But it was a large game and she didn't recognise very much.

She knew what fire looked like though. There was a lot of it around.

She felt the ground shake beneath her and was knocked down by something she couldn't see. She landed face down and rolled over to see something very large and very scary above her. Long neck. Wings that beat the air with such force she'd been literally unable to stand it. Teeth like the tusks of an elephant and feet talons the size of her head, all topped off with a fiery breath that ignited the trees around her and filled the air with ash and smoke.

Was that a dragon?

Those around her certainly seemed to think so. They swore about it volubly and the air was thick with their arrows. Between the flames coming down and the smoke and arrows going up, it was a wonder there was any air left to breathe.

She couldn't breathe enough of what was left and sank to the ground, coughing. Less than ten yards away, the dragon landed with a thump that she could feel in her teeth and moved towards her with all the inevitability of cynicism.

Debbie watched its approach with eyes wide but little focus: they were blinded by her tears. She still coughed with gusto.

And through her streaming eyes, she saw an impressionist retelling of Beowulf or St George. Here was the enormous predatory beast, making a meal of the innocent, although she didn't count herself in that number. She never had. Innocence was the opposite of guilt as well as guile, and she thought she had quite a lot of both.

And there, dressed as some kind of Viking and swinging a battleaxe that must have been bigger than her, was the titular hero. It was a mighty weapon and the edges of its blade danced with fire. Each time he hit the dragon, its wounds burned.

Debbie wasn't sure about the benefits of this in battle. Wouldn't that cauterise the cuts it caused, make them more likely to heal without infection?

But the axe was certainly doing the job. The dragon howled with pain and switched its attention to its assailant, slashing away at its wings.

The huge reptilian head turned to face the attacker, and with a forward tuck and roll, the large man dropped beneath it, appeared on the other side, leapt in the air, kicked himself off the wing, ran along the spine, made a huge jump with a blood-curdling roar, spun ninety degrees towards the dragon and brought the enormous axe down on the beast's neck. This man was a mystery. He had the fluid, balletic grace of a parkour enthusiast but the practical approach to problem solving of a butcher. His axe was stashed on his back before he hit the ground.

The head fell crashing down, bounced on the jawbone and landed two feet from Debbie, smoke still drifting from its nostrils.

She screamed and backed against the tree as the dragonblood pooled around her feet and splashed against her legs.

In the crowd of archers and fighters that had formed, many people covered their eyes and looked away from her. They knew what was coming and wanted to be spared the sight of it.

Debbie had no idea. She still had her eyes closed herself. After a couple of seconds she opened them and saw a crowd of people who still had theirs closed and were gesticulating strangely. Were they chanting?

They were. They were chanting and they were mournful. One walked over, priestly robes seeming to shimmer in the heat haze that still covered this area, and prepared the sacrament.

When he saw that Debbie was still alive, he looked absolutely terrified. So did the others.

The one that had killed the dragon didn't look scared, though. He looked thoughtful. Then, being careful not to actually touch her, he threw a sack over her head, tied her up with ropes and lashed her to the back of his horse.

Then he rode through the trees towards the palace. People would need to hear about this, and she might be worth something.

* * *

Debbie felt the bumps of the road in her hips, her spine, even in her shoulders and elbows. Shit, she felt it in her fingers. In her hair. She had no idea where she was going. She was still in a sack tied to the back of a horse.

She'd had no luck at all in trying to work out what had happened. She'd arrived here, as per her own intentions, but 'here' wasn't where she thought it would be. Previously, she'd started out in a nice harmless field.

Her first memory of this place would be the bird's eye view of the mud on her face when the beating of a dragon's wings had knocked her to the ground.

She hadn't seen much since then. She'd been choking from the fire for much of the time she hadn't actually been in the sack and her eyes had been watering like crazy. All she had were blurry shapes to base her memories on. She did remember seeing the dragon, though, as it flew over her. Her eyes had still worked properly at that point, apart from the mud in them.

It was enormous. It must have been at least forty foot long, probably about six feet across at the waist, the wings must have been a good fifteen foot each and the whole kit and caboodle must have weighed several tons.

How in the world did it get off the ground?

This train of thought was derailed suddenly as the horse stopped and she rolled painfully towards the rider. The armour was not especially accommodating. She thought she might now have a nose bleed as well.

Voices now. Officious. Sounds like a guard.

"Halt in the name of the Lord of Stonegard! Who goes there?"

"You know me, guard. I am Katerina, Keeper of the Lord's Gift, heir to the House of Wax and Champion of Tamara. Now, move out of my way or I'll have you whipped."

"I'm sorry, my lady. I didn't see you very well. We've had a lot of visitors tonight. Word in the tavern is that there's a dragon about."

"Not any more. I killed it, down by the lake. I'd forgotten about that. Thanks for reminding me. Send the miller to pick up the bones and the skull. I may make soup." She gave the guard a handful of gold coins from a bag at her waist and he took off his helmet and bowed to her.

She slapped his head on the way up.

"Never take off your helmet when you're on duty. Never let your guard down. This city has enemies everywhere. Be vigilant!"

"Yes, milady."

She rode on.

Behind her, still bouncing on a horse's arse, Debbie reflected on this. She was a woman? And she'd just decapitated a fire breathing dragon? She seemed to be quite an impressive woman.

The city was reasonably large and well established. The original settlers were fortunate to have found a place close to the river (it actually ran through the city) with a convenient forest and stone quarry. That was hundreds of years ago. Now there were mines dotting the landscape, farms, stables... Stonegard was a city that worked.

It worked most of the time, anyway. There were always those who weren't satisfied with that produced locally. Everything was more attractive if it came from further away. It was a bizarre situation. Lord and ladies of the city would host banquets where they would eat peasant food from the other side of the map, food that the locals had to eat because their lords and ladies had taken all the good stuff first.

Some of the most exquisitely spiced sauces came from countries where people had to make rice taste as nice as possible because someone else had had all the meat. But because everything was imported, at great risk and great cost, the local nobles spent more on a single meal than most families could live on for months.

So there had to be trade with the other city states of this region. The fancy ingredients of a fancy lifestyle had to be procured. Spice caravans made the long trip from the east. Silks too, became popular. There had been experiments done to produce something similar using the large brutish patriot wasps that were so proud of their homeland, they never seemed to want to go anywhere else, but they weren't successful experiments. There was probably psychological warfare potential to their venom, though, if it could be farmed. Being stung had turned many researchers into almost bald, gorilla-like thugs, bitter and resentful about the bees (that were actually far more useful and productive) that had made their homes here. Get enough venom inside one of the competing city states and it would tear itself asunder as it turned on itself.

59

So far, though, like the idea of indigenous silk, bananas, chilies, ginger or drinkable wine, it was not an idea that had gone anywhere.

They did have the climate for good whiskey, though. Much of the city had risen on the whiskey dollar. In a time before technology, drinking was the main form of entertainment. Gods knew the bards and minstrels were pretty shit.

* * *

The doors to the palace were high and wide, so Katerina just rode straight in, the hooves of her burdened mount echoing loud on the stone flags. At the end of the long room were the three thrones.

On the left was the Keeper of the Lord's Peace. It was a position somewhere between police commissioner and field marshall, MI5 and MI6. The Peacekeeper had a network of spies that stretched far beyond the realm of Stonegard. His job was as his title implied: to keep the place peaceful. Whether this meant putting down the occasional rebellion, defending the borders, or indeed extending them, made little difference to him. He was a man without much sentiment. It was a job that had always been given to the practical type.

On the right was the Keeper of the Lord's Bounty. This was something akin to a modern chancellor of the exchequer, although the modern day ministries of agriculture and housing would also be part of his remit. He was ultimately responsible for making sure that everyone got fed and housed to an adequate standard, although it was of course him that defined what that standard was. This could have made the job rather easy for him. He was also responsible for ensuring that trade continued to flow through the city, that citizens and the occasional merchant were taxed, and that the Keeper of the Lord's Peace had enough money to enforce the payment of those taxes. The Lord had been known to get less than peaceful were that not the case.

And in the middle was the Lord himself. His throne soared above him, a patchwork mosaic of dragonbone and gold. His name was Gosbert III and he was angry.

"What do you mean, bringing your horse in here? This is not the stable of some whorehouse. This is the Throneroom of Stonegard and my court has a right to more respect than this."

"Apologies, my lord, but time is pressing. I think I may have found the Dracomorph."

There was some laughter. "Katerina, this is nonsense," said the Lord's Bounty. "There is no truth to those old prophecies. A woman, born of a monster, who can withstand the blood of a dragon, a woman who indeed contains the blood of a dragon, blood that would burn the flesh from anyone else? A woman who can actually turn into a dragon? These are tales told by an idiot, full of sound and fury. I'm afraid they don't signify very much at all."

"And yet this very day, when I was slaying the dragon, I saw a woman soaked in the blood of the beast. She lived."

"And where is this miraculous woman?" asked the Lord's Peace. "Did she turn into a dragon and fly away?"

"No, she's in the sack tied behind me." And Katerina slapped the hessian bag. There was a muffled yelp.

"Are you insane?" asked the Lord of Stonegard, getting to his feet. "You have found who you believe to be the Dracomorph, the culmination of a thousand year prophecy and a woman of unspeakable power, so you put her in a sack and tied her to your horse's arse?"

"I never said I was a diplomat," said Katerina.

"Just as well," murmured the Bounty sardonically.

"I don't suppose there is any truth whatsoever to your story," said the Lord, scratching his beard. "But I'd be a fool not to check it out. Take her to the wizard. This is a magical matter and that is his affair."

"As you wish, my lord," said Katerina, as she turned her horse around and headed towards the alchemy tower.

* * *

Like Debbie, Peter was trying to work out what to think. He was new to the game.

He'd landed here, in this forest. Well, it felt like landing anyway. He'd felt himself approach the ground, braced for impact and then seemed to be upright in a body he'd never seen before.

There was a lake over there. Maybe he should have a look at his reflection.

He walked over, marveling at all the strange plants on the bank. One of them even seemed to be singing. Bizarre.

He crouched down and looked at the still waters, some small fish swimming below.

He didn't look bad as such, but he certainly didn't look like Peter. His cheekbones were high and proud, almost Asiatic. His hair was dark and short, close cropped to the top of the forehead. He was wearing some kind of armour that may have been made of leather but seemed to glow. And his ears rose to points.

Yeah, it looked like he was an elf. Cool. What could elves do?

Elves could do many things, depending on where you heard about them. Tolkien considered them almost immortal warriors, a revered, civilised and powerful race that were a large part of the history of Middle Earth. Perhaps uniquely amongst those with power, they gave it up and went into voluntary retirement, rather than holding on 'til the bitter end, regardless of the cost even to themselves, as humans are wont to do.

Elves in the Skyrim game, high elves at least, were generally feared and hated by the locals, who they looked down upon. It was commonly believed that they had used their magical and political wiles to force an empire into doing their bidding. They acted much as America did, insisting on their own superiority, abducting those who disagreed or questioned them and torturing them in secret, although these secret locations tended to be up in the mountains and not in the middle of someone else's desert.

Unknown to Peter, elves in Stonegard were more similar to those in Skyrim. When the miller and his sons had brought their cart round to the lake to pick up the dragon parts for Katerina, they had seen Peter and knew what they had to do.

There was a bounty on elves in Stonegard.

The miller raised his finger to his lips and pointed to one of his sons, then pointed ahead. The son nodded. His other son followed his instructions on the opposite side of the tree.

Peter now rested against that tree.

At a signal from their father, the two sons moved into position. One went for the legs, one the arms. Within seconds, Peter was manhandled to the ground with a rag in his mouth and a bag over his head.

"Nice one, boys," said the miller. "Well done for taking him alive. The wizard will give us a pretty penny for this one."

They threw Peter into the back of the cart, the bag falling from his head in the process. He looked up and gasped like a man with a rag stuffed in his mouth. He was lying next to the dragon's head. The teeth in its jaw towered next to him, those imperious nostrils soared above and the ears seemed to be a very long way away indeed.

This beast was enormous. What sort of world had he come to?

* * *

Katerina untied her prisoner from the back of her horse, removed the sack, cut loose the ties that bound her feet, and dropped her more or less roughly into the mud.

"Ow!" cried Debbie. "That hurt!"

"Can't be helped," said Katerina.

"Well, it probably could," said Debbie. "You could, for example, have left me as I was. I was no threat to you. Why did you put a sack over my head? Where are we anyway?"

Katerina looked surprised. "We're in Stonegard. Don't you recognise the place?"

Debbie looked around, getting used to having eyesight again. "No, I don't think I've ever been here before in my life."

"Are you sure?" There was some disappointment in her voice. The Dracomorph was believed to have come from these parts. If this woman was a stranger here, maybe she wouldn't be the Dracomorph.

"Fairly sure. I think I would have remembered living in a land that contained dragons."

"So where are you from?"

"A place called Harold Hill in Essex."

"Essex?"

"You probably haven't heard of it."

"No," said Katerina. "Who is your lord?"

"I don't think I've really got one."

"Oh, come on! Everybody has a lord."

"Everyone except me, apparently..." Debbie felt this was something else she'd been missing out on.

"Anyway," said Katerina, "we have a wizard to meet. And I'm afraid he will expect you to be quiet. He can be a bit cranky. So, if you don't mind..."

And she reached over and gagged her.

They climbed the stairs to the alchemy tower.

* * *

"Got an elf for you."

The guard looked down from the steps at the miller. "Just the one? Jarod came in with four yesterday, and he's as old and fat as my wife's mother. And my wife's not much better!" He chortled. They didn't high five in Stonegard but he clanged the armour of his forearm against that of his mate. He laughed as well.

The first guard started rummaging through his coin purse. "OK, two gold pieces as promised. Throw him on the pile with the others." And he gestured behind him. There was quite a mound building up.

"I think you misunderstand me. This one's alive."

"What? You caught a live one?"

"Yep. I think that's twenty gold pieces, isn't it?"

"Well, that depends. We'd have to look at the condition of it, wear and tear, that sort of thing. You know they lose 60% of their value as soon as you take them out of their homeland..."There was another clank of the armour.

"Come on, son, I ain't got all day," said the miller. "I've still got to drop off the dragon bones to Lady Fancypants. And I do have a mill to run..."

"Only joking, Therod. You'll get your money." It took both guards taking off their gauntlets but they counted out the twenty pieces.

"Cheers, lad. I'll take him up to the wizard. Your mum still like those cakes young Cyrol makes? I can drop her some off later. I need to give Cyrol a batch of flour."

"My mum eats anything she can get her hands on."

"Course she does, the dirty cow," said the other guard. He went to do the armour clanking again but it hurt a lot more without the actual armour.

The miller shook his head as he led Peter up the stairs. "Welcome to the madhouse, mate," he said.

"I think I might have been here before," said Peter.

* * *

The wizard looked at Debbie critically. Then he walked towards her, held her mouth open, repositioned the gag and started feeling her teeth. She wished she had the use of her hands, or that her knees weren't tied together. If she could lift one without the other, the old wizard would know exactly how she felt about this examination.

"Hmmm," he said, holding her bottom lip and pulling it down for inspection. "I would have expected the Dracomorph to have bigger teeth. These are quite large, of course. But I don't think it's her." He replaced the gag, leaving Debbie glowering.

Katerina seethed under her breath. This girl could be worth something if this old quack would just give her the seal of approval. He was the Keeper of the Lord's Wisdom, a grand vizier sort, and he had influence here. Some, at least. Like a poet in the modern age, he was considered quite good at something that most people had no use for, but they kept him around just in case. But there was still suspicion. Magic, wisdom, literacy: somebody had to do them, and it might as well be old Wysbern. But round here, they still preferred an axe in their hand to a quill.

"Perhaps," said Katerina, "you could test that she is invulnerable to dragonblood, as I have seen."

"Alas, I have no dragonblood," said Wysbern.

"You're in luck. She's got some all over her feet and legs."

The old wizard pulled up her robes to investigate. Again, Debbie wished she was able to use her legs. His head was at foot height. It seemed ungrateful not to kick it.

"This looks like normal blood to me," said Wysbern.

"That's probably because it's dried and lost its potency. I saw it come from the neck of a dragon that I killed, hence the reason I believed it to be dragonblood."

"Hmmm..."

"OK, look. You know the legends of the Dracomorph as well as anyone. Do you believe that they themselves contain the blood of a dragon?"

"I believe that that's what the legends tell us, yes."

"So if this woman contained the blood of the beast, you'd accept she was the Dracomorph?"

"I suppose I would consider it."

"Right then." And she grabbed the wizard's wrist, pulled it over, whipped out her dagger, stabbed Debbie lightly in the finger and let one drop of blood fall on the wizard's hand, on the flap of wing-like skin between the thumb and forefinger. It bore right through. He howled in pain.

Then he held his hand up to the light. There was a small hole, the exact size of a drop of blood, and the edges of the wound were steaming.

"Did you just stab me?" he said in umbrage.

"No, I stabbed her," said Katerina. "I just dropped some of her blood on you." She held up the blade. "There's some left. Want some more?"

"No, I think you've made your point. This woman has unusual blood."

"Yes, she has the blood of the Dracomorph," said Katerina, getting cross.

"Well, that remains to be seen," said the wizard, going back to his investigation of this promising new subject. He pulled back Debbie's hair and peered into her ear. "If nothing else, we can farm her blood for poisoning arrowheads. But I would like to have a look at the skeleton when we're done, see if there were any signs of wings, that sort of thing. My experiments are progressing well."

He beamed, although they didn't seem to be going that well. It was hard to be sure what he was trying to achieve, but if he wanted a few cages full of amputees and a pile of corpses outside his window, he was doing very well indeed.

"Are you planning on doing to her what you did to all these, then?" said Katerina. "Wouldn't a live dracomorph be more useful?"

"Oh, I don't want to kill her. I didn't want to kill any of these, to be honest. But they have served the cause of magic and so will this one."

"I didn't bring her here to die. I brought her here because I wanted to know if she was the Dracomorph. I think I've got my answer."

"No, you brought her here for your reward, just like you always do. Well, here it is. Our business is done." And he gave Katerina a purse full of gold coins and a diamond.

She avoided Debbie's eyes when she left.

* * *

The wizard was still investigating Debbie when the miller arrived.

"Yes?" said the wizard. "I am engaged in a most subtle experiment at the moment. It cannot be interrupted except for matters of great importance."

The miller looked around. Subtle experiment? To the untrained eye, it just looked like an old man fiddling with a young woman, bound and gagged. Not much subtlety to that.

"Apologies, my lord," said the miller. "I have a live elf for you. The guards asked me to bring him up."

"Oh, well done. I know they can be tricky. This will be very useful. I like to see them before they die."

Shame you're in such a rush to make them die, thought the miller. But he just put Peter in the cage he'd been told to and went on his way. He did still have lots to do.

Peter looked through the bars and wondered what the hell he'd got himself into. What was going on here? It was like what he imagined the early days of anatomy to be like. Butchers with some basic medical experience cutting up a different type of meat, trying to figure out how it all worked.

Perhaps he'd have been the same, if he'd been around back then. If there was nobody actually doing the experiments, grisly though they were, modern medicine would not have advanced as far as it had.

And here? He had a look around him. It didn't seem like it had advanced very far at all.

That tool the wizard is holding doesn't look very clean. Or very sharp.

Debbie agreed with Peter and complained loudly when the wizard tried to get some blood for himself. She had managed to spit out the gag.

"Don't move so much, girl. It's just a tiny **prick**..."

"And I suppose you'd know all about tiny pricks, wouldn't you?" she said. "You look like you'd be a world authority on the subject."

Peter chuckled. The wizard turned on him.

"Laugh now, elf. When I'm done with this one, you're next."

Peter watched him through the bars of his cage.

Oh good.

Something to look forward to.

* * *

Elitism was an interesting and sometimes misunderstood concept. There were essentially two types, the political/social and the intellectual/practical. Or to put it another way, the 'who you know' and the 'what you know'.

They knew about elitism in Stonegard. They all believed in different types for different reasons, or perhaps for the same reason. They all believed in the type of elitism that put them in the elite.

Lord Gosbert III believed that, because he was son of Lord Gosbert II, he had the right to rule this city. Clearly he had the blood of a lord coursing through his veins and what better proof was there than that? Even if he didn't just magically inherit his father's wisdom and abilities (many stupid children had smart parents, and vice versa), he had been around power all his life. He wasn't just born to power, he'd been trained for it. Each time his father told him something else about the world, each time the son of another local noble came to his childhood birthday parties, he was forming the bonds and gaining the experience necessary to run Stonegard.

Therod the miller believed in the practical approach. He believed he should be miller because he was the best person for the job, he had the most experience of milling, and, rather crucially, he had a mill. It would be hard for the fisherman or the goatherd to produce flour as well as him, therefore he should be in charge of that side of things. This is part of the 'meritocracy' side of elitism, the belief that it should be skill, ability and experience that drives someone to the top, but there was a bit of social elitism too. He had a mill because his dad used to have a mill, then he'd died. And like Gosbert, he'd learnt his father's trade at his father's knee.

And Katerina just sat in the tavern nursing her mighty tankard and wondering where she fit into it all. She had titles, sure. She was 'heir to the House of Wax', but in practical terms, it just meant she inherited her mum's candle shop when she died. She was 'Champion of Tamara', but that was because she did a favour for a priestess once. It could only be an honorary title.

And she was 'Keeper of the Lord's Gift', which did mean something. She had a small parcel of land on the outskirts of town. This was a city that still tried to reward noble deeds with noble titles. Or at least it had been then, when Gosbert II was still alive. He'd seen that she'd been doing some favours for his people, saw that it was for the good of the realm and rewarded her.

Many titles were once bequeathed in such a manner. Somebody would fight well in battle, or lend a king a horse so that he could, and they would be rewarded with half of Buckinghamshire. And once you had the land, you had the serfs, you had the income, and seven hundred years later, your descendants would imagine that they were somehow better than those whose ancestors didn't have a spare horse at the exact time some ancient and forgotten king had wanted one.

As someone who had actually earned the title herself, though, Katerina was proud of having the Lord's Gift. There were only a few in the city to hold such an honour.

Someone who has achieved nobility through their own acts is more likely to be genuinely noble than someone who has merely inherited it. They have shown themselves to be capable of it. And it was this nobility of spirit that so troubled Katerina now.

She really wasn't happy about leaving Debbie with that wizard.

* * *

Natasha heard the bleep and looked up. That was Peter's timer going off.

She went back into the computer room and watched his consciousness flood into his face. That was a relief.

"How you feeling?" she asked.

He looked around, getting his bearings. "Not so bad, thanks. That was a strange place."

"Did you enjoy your life as an elf?" When she'd first met the players in the game, Ken had been an elf, and so had Debbie. Unfortunately, he was a wood elf, she was a dark elf and the two didn't normally play well together. To be fair, though, she did stop setting him alight when she regained her identity. Unfortunately, too, 'Throne of Dragons' spanned an entire continent of warring city-states. Stonegard had not been as accommodating of elvenkind as the sylvan glades that Natasha had seen.

"Enjoy it? Not massively, no. Did you know they hunt elves there?" he asked.

"Really?"

"Yes. They pay a bounty on them."

"Sorry, I had no idea. Ken was more involved with this game than I was. I'd always assumed that elves would get a bit of respect."

"Not noticeably, no."

"Well, you got back safely at least. Did you discover anything useful when you were in there?"

"Well, there was this old wizard who seemed to be experimenting on a young woman. I was next on the slab, apparently. They put me in a cage."

She thought for a moment. "The system usually puts you where you need to go. What else did you see?"

"Not a great deal, to be honest. I seemed to fall from the sky, then I had the body of an elf. I checked my reflection in the lake. Pointy ears and everything. Then I was getting my bearings when two brutes tied me up and threw me in a wagon with what looked disturbingly like a dragon head. After that, they took me to a castle and put me in a cage."

"Hmmm. I've a hunch you were close to something important though."

"Yes, I know what you mean. I had the strongest feeling that there was something there I should have been doing."

"I think you're right. Mission objectives often come out as a sort of reprogramming of the subconscious." She looked at him. "You want to go back?"

"Yes, I think I should."

"Alrighty then. Re-immersing in 10, 9, 8..."

* * *

Strange things were afoot in the wizard's tower.

When Peter had left the game, the elf he'd bodyjacked had come back to his senses. The personality of Quendor, priest of the Ecliptic Dawn, was back home again, and he didn't like what people had been doing to the place.

Last thing he remembered, he was strolling through a forest, keeping an eye out for bounty hunters. He shouldn't have too many problems: he had a good stock of invisibility potions. They'd helped him out before.

Then the elf had found himself here, in a cage, watching an elderly man poke and prod a young woman, who he seemed to have tied up. Was this some kind of bondage dungeon? What in the name of Elrond Hubbard was going on?

"You there! Unhand that woman in the name of..."

And then he stopped dead. His pointing finger stopped quivering, his head started to vibrate from side to side, then his whole personality seemed to change. His leg muscles worked differently and his weight shifted. He stood straighter and instantly seemed calmer than he had been. In fact, he seemed to have no recollection whatsoever of how angry he'd been a second ago.

He looked in puzzlement at his outstretched arm and lowered it slowly to his side.

Wysbern stopped looking at Debbie and looked at Peter, just one more British soldier re-occupying something he'd already occupied some time before.

"How dare you! This is a delicate magical experiment! You could have seriously impeded my progress!"

"How dare I what?" said Peter, in his normal voice. He had none of the elf's accent.

Now Wysbern paid more attention. "Interesting. I had theorised that elves were subject to demonic possession, because of their pointy ears. They act as receivers, you know, for psychic energy. I shall probe you thoroughly."

"Excuse me?" Then he remembered he was an elf. "Er..." He had no idea what to say. Elves? That wasn't really his thing. "I'm sure you would know better than I," said Peter quietly.

"So much for the pride of the elves," muttered Wysbern wryly. "Yes, I do. And you would do well to remember it."

He went back to poking Debbie.

Then the door opened.

"Ah, Katerina!" said the wizard. "What miracles of nature have you brought for us this time? Have you found some wondrous cat that can turn into a caterpillar? A horse that can turn into lasagna? This girl is no more a dracomorph than I am. You couldn't find a one-eyed trouser snake in a whorehouse."

"Whatever she is, she's not yours," said Katerina. "I'm giving you your money back. What you're doing isn't right."

"What I'm doing, wench, is keeping this kingdom safe. What I'm doing is making damned sure that this 'dracomorph' doesn't exist, because if it does, somebody else might get it. And if I find it, I'm going to kill it. How do we even know we can control it?"

"What you are doing is satisfying whatever sick need you have to see what people look like on the inside. If you

don't stop doing it, the next guts you see will be your own."
She drew her sword. "These two are coming with me."

"But you only paid for one of them!" cried the wizard,
as his two latest and most promising specimens were led
from his tower.

* * *

"Can you ride?" Katerina called over her shoulder to
the others.

"No," said Debbie.

"A little," said Peter, "but I'm rusty."

Katerina rolled her eyes. "You're not making it easy to
be noble, you know."

"Sorry!" said Debbie. "I don't come from somewhere
that has many horses."

"OK, you, girl, get behind me. Elf, you're on your own.
Keep up if you can but I'm not going to be able to wait."

"Business as usual then," said Peter gloomily. He had
mounted the horse: his elven form had none of the
problems a man of his age might have had in the real world.
Now he held the reins and tried to remember what to do.

"Tally ho, then," said Katerina and geed her horse into
action.

"Right behind you," said Peter, and squeezed the horse
with his calves. OK, this was coming back to him. The
horse was at least moving now, although slowly. Katerina
was some distance ahead of him.

Still visible though. He could still catch her if this stupid
beast would move its arse a bit quicker.

Now he thought back to his riding experiences. There
weren't that many of them, but a girl he'd been interested in
at uni was a keen rider and he wanted to impress her. So
he'd taken a few lessons, then she found a boyfriend and he
lost interest.

He never imagined there would be a time when his life would depend on his equestrian prowess.

But he knew he had to get this thing moving faster at least. He squeezed in his legs some more.

OK, now we're cooking, trotting along nicely. There was something he had to remember about the trot, wasn't there? The horse moved its legs diagonally, so he had to rise in the stirrups every step... he nearly fell... OK, every other step and there was something he had to remember about turning as well. Oh shit, he'd better remember quickly, that tree doesn't look like it's going to move. I'm pulling the reins, you stupid horse! No, don't just turn your head, turn your body – you're still going forward... Jesus, what was it...

He tried to imagine the horse as a motorbike, and leant towards the left: maybe that would work here. No, he just felt himself falling off. He frantically tried to hold on with his knees and the horse started to change direction.

He began to figure this out logically like the doctor that he was. It wasn't the change of balance that had made it turn, it was when he'd panicked and his knees had tightened. He'd been sliding to the left, so he'd tried to hang on more with his right knee and the horse had been trained to expect it. They did say something about that at the stables, didn't they? When turning left, apply more pressure to the right of the horse.

Well, it seemed to have worked.

Phew.

He was still too slow, though. Katerina was a long way ahead. How did he canter? Purely out of desperation, he gave it a whack with his heels and it was off, thundering through the trees.

Now he just had to avoid those trees, which seemed a lot closer together at this speed. He gritted his teeth, leant forward on the horse and flew through the forest like an Ewok on a hot-wired jet-bike.

* * *

The hills of Stonegard were pounded by the hooves of many horses. Katerina and Debbie had taken the lead, Peter was doing his best to catch up, and way too close behind him but approaching rapidly were six knights of the Lord's Guard.

He looked back and wished he hadn't. Firstly, he nearly lost his balance again and secondly, he saw the weapons.

They were not sophisticated weapons. They had originally been used for threshing, then weaponised. All the knights were riding one handed and brandishing a flail, a large spiked ball attached by a chain to a handle. But it was certainly effective. From the Japanese nunchaku through the Depression-era coshes and blackjacks to Charles Bronson's 'sock full of quarters' weapon from the Death Wish franchise and the flailing handbags of Monty Python's little old ladies, it had always been known how much quicker something can travel if it's allowed to be flexible. This is part of the reason that sperm are able to reach the egg: they use their tails to whip themselves forward. And it's the reason whips make a noise when you crack them. It's not the sound of one part of it hitting another. It's the sound of a sonic boom as the tip breaks the sound barrier.

Peter knew how much damage these weapons could cause, especially when their forward momentum was added to the speed of the horse, which would have to be travelling quicker than him to have reached him in the first place.

He would have to see that they didn't.

"Come on!" he cried to the horse, digging in his heels. But he was starting to lose hope a little. He couldn't really ride and he was struggling to stay in the saddle. He also suspected that this horse would be stolen. As far as he was aware, he didn't have one. They'd been in the stables and this horse was just there, ready to go. He supposed his mysterious rescuer could have procured a horse for him, but it seemed unlikely. He didn't feel like he figured in the equation at all. It was all about the girl.

What was so special about her? And what was this 'Dracomorph'?

An arrow went pinging past his head. So they didn't need to catch up with him after all.

Great.

He leant forward as far as he could and whipped the horse's neck with the reins.

"Faster!" he urged. "And I'll buy you a carrot the size of your penis..."

The guards behind continued to accelerate and the horse ahead continued to recede. Then, it seemed to stop. Peter strained his eyes. Was he getting some help after all?

The girl had fallen off. She was the priority, apparently. That female knight is getting off her horse to help her. Typical, thought Peter. She didn't even slow down for me.

Now she's bending over her. With her sword out? Didn't she want to save her?

She did. A couple of hundred yards ahead, she was bending over Debbie, investigating her wounds. She had cut both arms when she'd fallen, one of them pierced by a low branch. There was a lot of blood.

"I was hoping you'd bleed," said Katerina. "Now we've got a chance." She knelt down, sword in hand.

"What are you going to do to me?" asked Debbie. She was still winded from the fall, she hadn't tried getting up yet, she seemed to hurt everywhere she could think of and she still had part of a tree protruding from her forearm. Now her noble rescuer seemed to have some very strange ideas about nursing. How did swords fit into it exactly?

"You are the Dracomorph. Your blood has power. I can use it against these bastards."

"You want my blood?"

"Not all of it. Just enough to coat my blade now and then. You would not believe how powerful it is. Keep it coming and we may get out of this."

Katerina put the flat of her blade against the wound, drew it back slowly, turned it over and did the same again. She held it to the light. It was steaming.

She nodded.

Debbie wasn't really happy with the situation. "So you're not going to heal me? You want me to just sit here with open wounds?"

"I'll heal you when we're done. I need your blood."

"Well, I kind of need it too! And it was mine first."

"If I don't get it, we're both going to die."

"And if you die, you can't heal me. What if you kill them all but die in the process? Then I'm just going to bleed to death, aren't I?"

Katerina looked at the horizon. Those knights were getting pretty close. "OK, fine, here's a healing potion, just so you know you can trust me. Don't take it until I stop needing your blood, OK? Either because they're all dead, or I am." She pulled out a dagger. "Take this as well. Imbue it with your own blood, and I promise you, it will be a whole lot more effective."

Debbie looked at this. It didn't look very clean. But she did have a healing potion. It looked like a perfume bottle and was full of some kind of liquid. What it actually did was anyone's guess.

Then she thought back to the first time she'd been in this world. She had been magically healed and she had drunk potions that would top up her own magical reserves. Maybe she could trust this Katerina woman. She did seem to want to help her.

"OK," said Debbie. "Be careful."

She had a look at the branch that still seemed to grow from her arm. It looked like it would be painful to remove. She moved it around a little, trying to work it loose, and there was another blossom of blood. But where her blood had touched the wood, it had already started to work. Debbie smelt burning, then watched in amazement as the visible part of the branch burnt at the bottom and just fell off. As she gently moved her arm from that which remained, a column of ash stood for a moment and vanished on the breeze.

Remember Me

Amanda Parker Adams

Rose knew this year might be the last. With James gone last fall and her arthritis getting worse, she knew. This year she enlisted her eldest daughter to make the trip, without explanation.

Marie sat behind the wheel, driving toward the Pacific Ocean. The sun was barely above the horizon an hour and just starting to warm up the sky. Reaching Half Moon Bay, Marie turned south on the Coastal Highway.

"Why are we going to the beach today? It'll be too hot out. Why not tomorrow?"

Ignoring her daughter's pleas, she remained quiet for a half hour.

"Pull in here, Marie. This is it," Rose said as they approached a small, unmarked parking lot on the side of Highway One.

Marie pulled the car into the dirt lot and helped her mother out of the passenger side. Barely a few spaces for parking, combined with a port-a-potty and a sign. Crop fields surrounded the small paved lot.

"I don't understand. Where are we, mother?"

"You don't have to understand. You just have to be here. This is the right time for you to know. I think James would have wanted this. I know he did."

"I don't see a beach, mom, only a service road heading nowhere."

"That's where we're going."

Rose used her floral umbrella as a walking stick as they started down the dirt road. It dipped, then curved to the left, opening up to a cliff overlooking the Pacific Ocean. Marie stood back where the road ended, watching her mother stare at the expanse of water. After a few minutes, Rose turned away from the water and walked toward the right side of the cliff.

"Come, Marie, let's go wiggle our toes in the sand."

Marie caught up to her mother, "But there's no san-"

Rose pointed at the cliff ahead of them. Marie noticed the steps her mother was pointing to. They were carved into the cliff, made firm by old railroad ties, leading down to a quiet, sandy beach. Reaching the last railroad tie, Marie noticed that high tide had washed out the last twenty feet some years ago. A rope guided them down an uneven path off to the left. Sitting down on a worn fallen log, they removed their shoes and buried their toes in the warming sand.

Rose dug her feet in deeper, finding something hard and smooth with her toes. Bringing it to the surface, she found it to be an old coke bottle, the kind Rose hadn't seen in decades. She removed the cork and pulled out a rolled up piece of vellum. She froze, realizing what she was holding.

Gently pulling the paper from her mother's hands, Marie began to read.

> *My lovely Rose Marie Byrne (formerly Rose Marie Parker). I hope you'll find this before I return from Europe. Remember when we courted? All of us coming here, but we used to sneak off alone. I'm leaving it here, hidden in a place on this beach that you and I always snuck off to. Here we are, husband and wife. This war in Europe will end soon. I will be home before you know it. Then we can start our life together.*
> *All my love,*
> *Arthur.*

Rose walked down to the water, wading in ankle deep. Warm on the surface, the water didn't provide the relief she desired. Marie walked up behind her mother, waves lapping at her toes.

"Who's Arthur?"

"Your father."

"Father died last fall," Marie took a step back, out of the water.

"James raised you, but he wasn't your biological father. Arthur was. Arthur and James were fraternal twins. In high school, James, Arthur, Betty and Joe, and myself, would all come down to this very beach on the weekends. The boys hauled firewood for a sunset bonfire. After graduation, the call came for young men to enlist. Arthur signed up first, despite protestations by their mother. He wanted to fight in Europe. We married a week before he left for basic training. He came home for a week before going to Europe. Weeks after he left, his battalion reached the beaches of Normandy on June 6, 1944."

"Wasn't that D-Day? Mom, how is it no one has ever mentioned Arthur?"

Rose didn't seem to hear her daughter's questions.

"Soon after Normandy, James got excited and enlisted in the Navy, defying his brother's wishes. The morning of July 23rd, I got the call from the doctor. I was pregnant with you. James, on furlough after finishing basic training, myself and all our family and friends came here to celebrate the impending baby and to see James off. Your Aunt Betty and Uncle Joe were still at the house. They received the telegram. They rushed here, forgetting the food back at the house. The telegram stated that Arthur had died on the beaches of Normandy. We found out later from a neighbor's son who survived, that it took weeks to locate and identify the dead."

Rose continued staring out over the water.

"The log wasn't here then. And those steps came all the way down. After an hour, James said he'd take his brother's place, if I was willing. He would be the father to my unborn child. We both knew it wouldn't be the same. Arthur was my soul mate. Nevertheless, I agreed. Raising a baby alone back then just wasn't done."

Rose stepped out into the water further, now with the waves lapping around her knees.

"James served his country and came home. You were eight by the time we had children of our own. Grief was something we kept private. James and I came back here every year on July 23rd, to remember Arthur."

Rose turned to look at her daughter. They stared at each other for a long while.

"This may be one of my last times."

"Mother, don't say that. You still have plenty of time."

"Not really. Do you remember the doctor visits the last several months?"

Marie nodded as Rose looked away.

"The official tests came back a few weeks ago, but I already knew what was happening."

Marie waded out to stand next to her, and took her mother's hand, "What is it?"

"I have Alzheimer's Disease. It progresses slowly, but I will lose my memories. Eventually, I will forget about Arthur. I wanted to bring you here this year to pass this on. So you know the truth. So that you know about your other father. The one who died for you."

Marie teared up, almost dropping the letter into the water.

"I always wondered why I didn't look that much like papa. Why didn't you tell me about this before?"

"Because James and I agreed not to. But then..." Rose looked back at her daughter, and then back out to the Pacific Ocean, "then James was gone. Too quickly. James knew before he died. About me. About my own illness. He tried too hard at times."

"All of those purchases he made those last few months. Those were for you. To help..."

"Yes. Memory cards, warning bells for when I might go wandering one day. Why he obsessively changed those smoke alarm batteries just to make sure I didn't burn the house down. And so much more."

The waves were getting stronger and Marie noticed they were affecting her mother's balance. She wrapped her arm around Roses' waist.

"I would never have been able to make this trip alone. But with James gone, and my memory slipping away, I wanted you to know the truth from me. I wanted you to understand why we did what we did. And why we protected you. Before it's too late."

"Mother, there are medications now. They can help you."

Rose waved her hand around, as she always did when dismissing something someone said, "No. Those will only delay the inevitable. There is no cure. Not in my lifetime, my child."

"But they would give us more time at least."

"No. I have made my own decisions, while I am still able. When we get home, we have some things to take care of. Maybe not today. But it must be soon. I have signed my part, but I need you to sign them as well. You may not agree with everything I have chosen, but this is how I want to live out my days. And end them."

Marie watched her mother, her arm still wrapped around Roses' waist. Wisps of her greying red hair came loose from the sloppy bun at the base of her neck, brushing against Roses' face. Rose closed her eyes, letting the warm air embrace the two of them.

"He knows," Rose said, her eyes still closed. She smiled and lifted her chin. "It feels like he's here. I never felt it before. I felt close to his memory all these years, but this year. I feel his strength." She opened her eyes and looked at Marie, "He would be so proud of you. James was, and he knew his brother would be as well, if he had lived. You have done so well for yourself, raising your daughters to be proud young women. Remember him for me, will you? Remember Arthur. I have a box of pictures of him. And letters that arrived even after his death. Before I knew- before they notified us. It sits on top of my curio cabinet in the dining room. Remember him for me, for James, will you?

Marie squeezed her mother's waist just a little tighter, "Of course I will mom, of course. Maybe we should get back to the log and have a rest."

"Yes, and let us bury our toes in the sand a little more."

Marie smiled. She had never seen her mother like this. They turned and walked back out of the water to dry sand. As they settled back on the worn out log, Rose turned to her daughter and noticed the rolled up piece of vellum in Marie's hand.

"What's that, my dear?"

"What?"

"That paper."

"This is the letter from Arthur," she said as she handed it to Rose. She read it silently, her lips moving but no sound.

"That's me! This is to me," Rose said, as she continued reading. "But who is this Arthur fellow, and why was he writing to me?"

Marie looked at her mother, the wisps of hair crossing the gently wrinkled face before her. A tear formed right in the corner of her eye. She fought to hold it back, but it was too strong. She had been too strong all these years. Too blind to see the frailty in her own mother, the woman who pushed her out in the world and helped her grow into the powerhouse she had become in her own life. Her silent guardian and cheerleader standing in the shadows her whole life. That person was slipping away right before her eyes. She wiped the tears away from her cheek and gently took the letter away from her mother, tucking it into her tote bag leaning against the log.

"Just some fella, mom. Some fella who loved you a long time ago."

She leaned in and kissed her mother on the forehead.

"Just like James. Just like me."

"Oh. Why are you wet?"

"We were out in the water, mother."

"Not your feet. Your face."

"It's nothing, mother. Nothing at all. I'm fine."

"Did that Johnny break your heart again? I keep telling you there's a better one out there."

"No. Johnny didn't break my heart. I broke his."

Rose smiled and laughed, "Good! He needs to know how it feels once in a while."

She didn't have the heart to tell her mother she divorced Johnny fifteen years ago, but she got two amazing daughters out of the deal.

Rose spotted the bottle the letter came in, "Well, look at this old thing. I wonder what it's doing out here."

"I'm sure someone left it behind for a reason, mom. Like maybe Arthur."

"Oh, I knew a fella named Arthur. Nice young man. I don't know what happened to him."

"Well, he-" Marie looked over at her mother again, brushing away her tears. "I heard something about him. He's in a better place now."

"Good, good. Why are we here again, Marie?"

"To remember things."

"I don't do so well at that anymore. Maybe you can help me remember."

"Yeah, mom. I can. I will. I love you, you know that, right?"

Rose nodded and leaned against Marie's shoulder.

"I'm not as quick as I used to be. We shouldn't stay too long. I'll need to get home to cook dinner for James."

"I'll get you home in time. I'll even help cook, okay?"

"Okay. We should go put our feet in the water."

Marie smiled, "Sounds like a great idea."

Chance Fortunes

A Story From Questworld

R.R. Virdi

He stirred his finger through the black ale in a lazy circle, waiting for bad luck to strike.

A chorus of cheers and ongoing applause caused him to shift on his stool. Turning from the bar counter, he watched bright orbs of fire tumble through the air. Each was no bigger than a fist, every one of them a different color than the next, a dizzying array of light and fire weaving through the air.

A woman twirled in the middle of the guild hall as she sent more balls of fire into the air. She directed them with nothing more than thought and deft motions of her body.

The screams intensified.

"Woo, Kheera!" slurred a balding man layered in ropes of heavy knotted muscle. His drink sloshed over his mug and onto the table as he continued shouting.

Her sarong fluttered as she twisted, its earthy hues of red, brown, and green, appeared to shimmer and blend under the firelight. One of the fireballs drifted close to a nearby guild member, who had to jump from their seat to avoid it.

Kheera paused, her bare midsection tightened as her breathing quickened. Everyone turned to stare at him.

He winced.

She adjusted her gray top and resumed the frantic, rhythmic dance. Kheera's lithe body contorted as she formed a strange pose with a dancer's grace.

Another ball of fire spun out of control. The purple orb impacted another member's shirt, setting it afire.

"Gyaaah!" The member batted at the flames with both hands, spilling his drink and worsening the situation. Two nearby men rushed over, threw him to the ground, and swatted him until the flames subsided.

Someone screamed. More followed. An entire table ignited as several balls landed upon it, sending up yellow, blue, and green flames.

"No, no, no!" Kheera stomped her feet, clapping her hands together, the flames died. Everyone turned to face him—again...

He swallowed.

Kheera stormed over to him. She was taller than the average man, looming over him as he hunched, shrinking his figure. Her tiny fists balled around the collar of his brown leather duster. She gave a sharp tug, bringing him level with her eyes. If he bothered to sit up straight, he'd be looking well over her head.

"Kheera, I—"

She cut him off with a growl. The rest of the guild watched in silent anticipation. "Chance, I have done that dance every year. Every year! Not once have I finished it perfectly. Why is that, Chance?"

"I can't control my magic, you know how it—" He waved his arms in feeble protest.

Kheera pulled her hands away, running them through her short cropped brown hair. Her brows knitted together. "Your magic," she said, scowling at the last word, "is a curse!"

Chance's shoulders drooped further, and his gaze fell to the floor. "I'm sorry," he mumbled.

Kheera released her grip on his coat and stepped away. Her lips twitched, but she said nothing.

Chance flinched as a weight fell on his shoulder.

If he stood at full height, the woman who had come up behind him would only come to his chest. Her dark hair was pulled into a single tail that fell to her shoulders. The woman's hand tightened on the meat between his shoulder and neck, giving him a reassuring squeeze.

"Leave him alone," she told Kheera, flashing Chance a sympathetic smile.

Kheera scowled. Pebble sized flames burst into existence. A dozen orbs spun in the air, colors blurring as they did. "Back off Aylia," warned Kheera.

The barkeeper's eyes hardened, becoming gray stone; her posture however, remained calm. Aylia tugged on the strings binding the apron to her body, she pulled it free, wiping her hands on it as she balled it.

Chance caught the apron as she threw it, gasping and letting it fall to the floor the second it touched his skin. A thin layer of frost blanketed the fabric. He looked to Aylia, whose fists clenched, pops ringing from her knuckles. He noticed the air around her hands become visible, like breathing on a cold winter's morning. The temperature plummeted around him and he swallowed again.

Oh no, he thought.

Aylia's hands were encased in solid ice, the tips of her fingers were tapered into frozen razors.

"Ladies..." said Chance. Both women whipped their heads towards him, glaring hard. His gaze promptly returned to the floor. Chance fumbled with his right hand, feeling near the counter. Gnarled, rough wood, brushed against his fingers. He gripped the wooden staff tight, shut his eyes, and began a silent prayer. Please don't let them fight, please don't let them fight. Stop it.

The ground shook. Kheera yelped. And Chance opened his eyes.

Ale leapt from every mug, suspended in the air above the room. Kheera's sarong caught fire. Aylia rushed to her aid, working to cool the flames.

"Oh no," muttered Chance as he clutched his wizard's staff to his chest. "Oh no, oh no, oh no...not again."

Frigid air poured out from Aylia's hands, subduing the flames on Kheera's clothes. The fire dancer shrieked as the sudden cold enveloped her legs. The flames died. Aylia jerked, pulling her hands away from Kheera—emitting a shriek of her own. The skin of her hands was red and raw. Kheera lay shivering, her color paling.

All members of the guild turned to face Chance, for the third time that evening.

He bounded up from the stool, hands waving to placate the mass of guild members. "I'm sorry. I'm sorry. You know how my powers are. Sorry, sorry. I...Kheera, I..." he trailed off.

"I'm going to kill him," growled Kheera, a fire burning in her eyes. She flexed her fingers, multicolored balls of fire erupted into existence.

Aylia's lips pulled away from her teeth as she snarled. "Not if I kill him first." In a gesture mirroring Kheera's, Aylia moved her fingers. A crystalline shell of sharpened ice encased her hands.

The ball of fire surged towards him. Chance dove aside as the fireball struck the counter, burned through it, and dissipated.

"My bar!" Aylia extended her arms.

"Sorry!" Chance clambered atop the counter, running as the chilling wave struck the spot where he had been. The ice formed overtop the wooden surface, overtaking him as he ran. He slipped. "Noooooo!"

Wood creaked, and cracked in protest as he hit two stools before impacting the ground. Chance couldn't tell if the spinning lights were more of Kheera's fires, if the world was spinning, or his head.

With his luck, he reasoned it was all three.

A gout of fire filled his vision. He winced and wrapped his coat around himself as a shield. Chance quivered, waiting for Kheera's fire to take him. It never came. He was left with chattering teeth as the temperature dropped. Chance opened his coat, the floor and counter behind him were covered in fresh snow. Cold mist hung in the air, the cause of his wet jacket. Chance's plucked a black lock of damped hair from his eyes, brushing it back along with the rest of his finger-length mane.

Using his staff, he pushed himself to his feat. "I'm sorry, Aylia, Kheera. I'm sorry!" he pleaded. A tingle filled his nostrils, his body bucked and lurched. He sneezed. Chance blinked, clearing his vision and sinuses. Both women stared at him in a mixture of anger and sympathy.

"I would have killed him you know? If you hadn't showered him in snow. Would have burned him well. Thanks..."

"Shut it Kheera. You couldn't crisp bacon."

Kheera stepped towards Aylia, her nose nearly brushing the other woman's face. Aylia took a step towards Kheera, both women's noses pressed against each other. Flames crackled back to life on Kheera's hands. Cold air circled Aylia's arms.

Chance sneezed again. A third of the ale that hung in the air above, fell. Chance moaned as the two women flinched, their bodies drenched in alcohol. He took a precautionary step back.

Both women turned slowly to face him, each arching a singular brow. They stared. An eye twitched for each women.

Every member in the guild inhaled, taking several long steps away from the enfolding scene.

A voice cut through the room like thunder. "What..."

Aylia and Kheera went rigid, their magic flared from sight.

Chance's stomach filled with snakes, his legs shook.

Oh...no.

She stood at top of the second floor staircase, looking down at the mess hall. Garbed in white, simple robes, she surveyed them all. Her face was lined with age, severity, and the scowl contorting her features. The elderly woman's hair was done into a tight, neat bun, just as white as her robes.

Her eyes were faded blue, slowly sifting over the entire hall, scrutinizing every member. And, she stood, at full height, no taller than Chance's waist.

"What," she repeated, her voice a whip crack that shook the entire building. "In the name of spaflunderous magic, is happening here?"

Chance bit his tongue, swallowing the urge to point out that, "spaflunderous," was not a word.

"I..." began Aylia.

"She..." Kheera pointed to Aylia.

"We..." both women said in unison.

Uh-oh, thought Chance. He turned, moving as slow as possible, creeping away from the scene. The air before him seemed to shimmer and fold. Oh no, not now. Please not now.

The remaining ale fell. No guild member was spared.

Chance sighed.

The old woman atop the stairs blinked. She comported herself, turning her focus to Chance. Her gaze narrowed. "Chance!" She snapped, the whole world shook again.

"Meep."

"Chance Fortunes, I should have known. Get up here. Right now!"

"Yes, guild master." He bobbed his head, searching for a safe path through the guild members. Every single one of them stared at him, intensely. Kheera and Aylia looks alone caused him to worry about his bodily safety. Chance tiptoed his way to the staircase, eyeing his fellow members warily as he did.

Taking the last step to the top, Chance stopped, bending at the waist. "Yes, guild master?" His voice came out higher in pitch.

The diminutive woman said nothing, turned on her heel and walked away.

Chance's long legs carried him to her side in a few quick steps. He remained silent as he walked beside the woman, fearing what an outburst from his mouth, or his magic, might incur.

The pair stepped through a set of wooden double doors, entering the room beyond. It was far larger than the space needed for a woman of that size.

Another thought Chance decided not to give voice to.

Shelves that touched the ceiling, ran wall to wall. Each was packed unceremoniously with books, tomes, scrolls and more. Bit of paper hung in random places within the shelves, some protruding from within the books, others, hanging wherever there was space. Her desk was simple in construction, solid black wood. Another mess of papers was spread across it.

And someone was sitting at it, their back turned to Chance.

Hair, the color of straw catching the sun at its height, hung down the middle of her back. She turned to face them.

In the stories, Chance would have sucked in a breath, awestruck by her youthful beauty.

He hated young people.

Fair skinned, with eyes much like the brown ale he'd sent spilling over the guild. When she saw them, she spread her mouth, sharing a wide, beaming smile.

Chance frowned, the pit of his stomach squirmed. He was going to be punished...somehow.

The young girl jumped from her seat. "Yes!" She shouted triumphantly.

"Sit!" barked the guild master.

The girl blinked several times in confusion before easing herself back into her seat.

"Sit," the guild master said in the same tone, pointing to an empty seat beside the girl.

Chance shut his eyes for a singular moment before complying. He settled into the seat, lifting his legs from the ground to keep them tangling over themselves in the low to the ground chair. The staff slipped from his grasp as he went to scratch his nose. He dove after it and missed. Chance struck the floor, hard. The staff clattered against one of the shelves.

He winced as he saw it happen.

A thunderclap sounded within the room. Everything occupying the shelves was thrown into the air as if a hurricane had blown through. Weighty books bombarded them, papers rained down throughout the room.

"Chance Fortunes! Can you not, for a single instance, cease to bring down misfortune, trouble, and sheer frustration?" The guild master quivered, the lines in her face hardening.

"I'm sorry Guild Master Pui-pui!" he muttered the apology as he fumbled for his staff, taking care not to bump another shelf as he did.

The young girl looked to Chance, and mouthed the words, Pui-pui.

His eyes widened and Chance shook his head in a gesture he hoped went unnoticed.

"That," said Pui-pui with a long sigh, "is my name."

The girl's mouth moved as if she were about to say something. She didn't.

Chance breathed out in relief. Smart girl, he thought to himself.

The elderly woman edged her way around the mess filled room, moving at a leisured pace to the other side of her desk. Once there, guild master Pui-pui took a seat, releasing a heavy breath as she did. Her lids fluttered, and seconds later, closed completely.

Chance and the young woman exchanged glances. He decided it best to wait, disturbing guild master Pui-pui was not conducive to a long and healthy life.

Her body jerked like she had been splashed with water, but the guild master's eyes remained shut. A cavernous exhale of air left her nostrils.

"Um, Guild Master?"

Pui-pui snapped straight, letting out a small groan. "What?"

"I, erhm, you fell asleep."

The guild master's eyes narrowed.

Chance's mouth ran dry.

"Chance, I am old, I am tired, I fall asleep. Dealing with heroes, great men and women in making, wizards and wonders...and those who fall short..." she paused, eyeing Chance. "It's all rather taxing."

He leaned forwards, sulking at her statement.

"Chance," she sighed. "You come a long line of great wizards, your mother was a particularly talented individual."

Chance nodded in silence at the comment.

"I see a bit of her in you, you have potential, but you also have a disastrous habit of being...a disaster. Honestly Chance, no member of this guild past or present, has the ability to cause such wanton destruction whether by intent, or accident, like you."

The brown of his leather boots caught his attention, they needed polishing. Chance continued to stare at his boots as the guild master spoke on about his ability as a wizard.

She sighed. "Chance, you have wonderful power, learn to use it properly, hm? To that end, I have an important job for you."

Something in the way she said important, put Chance on edge.

"This," she gestured to the young woman, "is—"

"Lillian Petals, happy to meet you!" She beamed, thrusting a hand towards Chance.

"Oh no, sorry," he said, inching away from her outstretched hand. "I don't." Chance was not overly fond of children — whether or not they were children was irrelevant. She was younger than him. Young people meant trouble.

The guild master cleared her throat.

His lips stretched as he forced the smile across his face. "Hello," his voice came out stone like, "nice to meet you." He wrapped his hand around hers, giving a gentle squeeze.

"Lillian has joined our guild, and is excited about taking up her first quest. Per guild rules, that mean's she needs a..."

"A guild guide," groaned Chance.

"Yes, and who better than one of the more renowned of our members? You've earned more money than handfuls of our members put together."

Chance looked to the floor once again, hoping this time it would swallow him whole. The guild master's statements weren't entirely true.

"This will be a wonderful learning experience for Lillian, a chance for her to earn some money, and see a bit of the world. As for you Chance, this an opportunity to develop better control over your peculiar magic and spend some time away from the guild. I have found that time away — a great deal of time in fact — can help one find a new perspective on things. Going on a quest with a new member will provide you time to reflect on things, Chance. To delve into your magic, and get you out of here. You don't want to be a chicken do you, cooped up in the guild, day after day?"

"No," he sighed.

"Spaflunderous! Take Lillian to the quest board, help her choose a quest suited to her skills and watch over her."

Chance suppressed the deep exhalation that wanted to leave his lungs.

"Out. Out," each word punctuated with a snap of the guild master's fingers. "I have work to do."

He inclined his head, rose from his diminutive seat and pulled his staff closer to his chest. "Come on Lillian, to the quest board."

Lillian leapt from her chair, sending her fist into the air in a gesture of triumph. "Wonderful, yes, thank you!" her tone carried all the enthusiasm Chance's managed to lack.

The girl sped towards the door, swinging it open and disappearing down the hall.

"You had best keep after the girl, Chance."

"Yes, Guild Master," his posture sunk as he said it. Chance took two long strides and was clear of the door, tapping it with the butt of his staff. The door shut with a soft thud. It was the sound that followed, that had Chance quickening his pace.

The ground tremored, sounding like something of giant weight had fallen in the guild master's office.

"Chance!" came the shout.

He found himself all-of-the-sudden, enthused over the opportunity to take Lillian on a quest and leave the guild for some time. It would be safer.

Chance descended the stairs, and found Lillian waiting for him. She stood stuck outside a handful of guild members huddling before a board the size of a table. Loose sheets of paper hung from it, held in place by a singular pin at the top, each sheet covered in writing.

Lillian bounced several times, vying for a better look at the board. "How much longer do I have to wait? I've been waiting for years to join a guild and start my first quest."

"A bit longer then," Chance commented.

Lillian tapped the shoulder of the nearest member. They ignored her. She tapped again, clearing her throat. As they turned, she spoke up, "Excuse me, I was wondering if for a moment, we could perhaps exchange places? I would very much like to look over the quest board, it's my first time you see." she flashed a sincere smile.

Oh no, thought Chance when he saw who Lillian was addressing. He nearly as tall as Chance himself, built like a reed that had sprung limbs and developed the temperament of a wasp. Dressed in overlaying patches of fabric that looked like algae and sodden earth, the slender man could easily have faded from sight in any forest. A quiver hung horizontally against the small of his back, equal in length to that of his hips. A mass of feathers arrayed in all manner of color, were visible at his back, contrasting the tones of his cloak. His fist was clenched around a bow noticeably smaller than that of average size.

The beanpole lowered his head, regarding Lillian from within his cowl, remaining motionless as he did.

"Um, please?" Lillian added.

Chance's knuckles ached from how hard he gripped his staff. Chips of ice had settled in his stomach, this could go badly.

With his free hand, the archer lowered his cowl. A wiry brush of black hair ran along his jaw and cheeks. His hair was cropped short and a shade of brown reserved for brightly polished wood, his eyes mirrored the color. A patch of skin the size of Chance's palm, directly below the man's right eye, was red and inflamed. Chance noticed a hairline thin stream of moisture trickle down the eye.

"New member huh?" the ranger's voice was silk over granite. "First quest, who's to be your guide?"

Lillian turned her head towards Chance. Her smile grew and she nodded in his direction.

The broomstick of man followed her gaze, took quick notice of Chance, and turned back. There was a second's pause before he performed a double take. When he recognized Chance, the man's knees shook, a shake that visibly made its way to his belly, back, and finally, his chest. He erupted into laughter.

"Chance? No Chance Fortunes? This is your guide?" his raucous laugh drew the attention of everyone within earshot. The ranger stumbled forward, placing a hand on a nearby wall for support. His chest continued to heave, tears formed and slid down his cheeks as his lips quivered in amusement. "Oh child, what manner of thing could you have done to anger our Guild Master to the point where she would appoint Chance - the living, breathing, magical disaster - Chance Fortunes, to be your guide?"

Lillian's smile slipped. She blinked several times, turning her head to Chance, searching him with her eyes.

Chance's knuckles whitened from gripping the gnarled and twisted wood of his staff. His teeth slid against each other. "Do not meddle in the affairs of wizards, especially the unlucky ones. They are not subtle, and bad luck comes in threes. Remember that, Kaeus."

The ranger's mouth moved absent words to follow. His tongue ran over his lips and Chance heard him swallow a bit of saliva.

"Walk away Kaeus," said Chance, struggling to level his voice in the unaccustomed hardened tone.

Everyone's eyes turned to Chance.

Kaeus found nerve and spoke, "Or you'll do what, Wizard of Misfortune?" He laughed. "The greatest threat you pose is to yourself!" He thrust his arms out to his sides, spinning in place.

Guild members burst into laughter.

Lillian's gaze fell to the floor.

And Chance's voice dropped to a hard whisper. He pointed the tip of his staff to Kaeus' rash inflicted eye, nearly touching it. "Or I'll use my power...with intent."

The laughter stopped.

Kaeus' hands flared to action as he waved them in a gesture to calm Chance. "Let's not be rash."

Chance arched an eyebrow. "No?"

Kaeus let out a weak laugh, looking to others nearby for support. "Chance, last time you used your magic in anger—the guild bedrooms caught fire, the ale turned to saltwater, a portion of the roof collapsed—followed by rain! Then there were the bees. We still have no idea where they came from! You wouldn't."

"Apologize to Lillian, walk away, Kaeus, and you won't have to find out."

Kaeus nodded in agreement. He muttered a quick apology and left.

Chance turned to face the remaining crowd. "Lillian would like to look at the quest board, please." When no-one showed sign of moving, he hoisted is staff and motioned to slam it to the ground. They scattered, deciding to find matters of greater import to occupy themselves with.

Chance did not turn to see them leave. "Are they... gone?"

"Yes Chance, they're gone," answered Lillian.

"Oh good," Chance collapsed against his staff, leaning on it for support. "That was hard! Kaeus is going to be mad— really mad."

A tight and unfamiliar weight wrapped around his body. "That was so brave! Thank you Chance!"

"Um, what are you doing?"

"Hugging you."

Chance took care in prying her arms from around his torso. "Um, there, there," he said, patting her on the head with each time he spoke. "I'm simply not comfortable hugging, or many other things that for that matter. Too much can go wrong with my powers."

"Chance?"

"Yes?"

"What are your powers exactly? I understand if you don't want to speak about them, but..."

Chance worked to force the weak smile across his face. "How about we choose your quest first, huh? After that, we can talk about my magic, and maybe more. Is that okay?"

"Yes, and thank you." she smiled.

He mumbled something incoherent under his breath.

Lillian sped past, her steps culminating in a joyous leap a few feet from the board. Her head bobbed as she scanned the dozens of jobs lining the board, an endless number of choices, varying in danger and reward. One piece of paper caught her eye, she leaned closer to study it. Her body quivered and she plucked the sheet from the board. "How about this one?" she pushed the sheet towards Chance.

Pinching the paper with thumb and forefinger, he plucked it from her grasp. "Hm." A thick dash made from charcoal, hung in the top right corner of the sheet, indicating the job's risk.

Safe for new members. He released a breath of relief. If Lillian had picked something higher, Chance would have been obligated to follow. She would not be denied more dangerous quests so long as she had a guide of higher standing with her. Chance was not overly fond of dangerous quests. Danger is adverse to one's longevity.

"So?"

"It could have been worse," he muttered.

"What?"

"It sounds like a great first choice, Lillian! Simple really. Find a few missing townsfolk, discover what happened, and return them home. Simple." he smiled. Of course more often than not, when someone goes missing, something has taken them. Oh dear.

"How far is Thistle town from here?"

"Depends. If I hire us a carriage, three days. Walking... farther. I like walking, however. Less complicated, much safer. You can never trust horses...at either end," he grumbled.

"Well there might be a better way to get there than any of those," she smiled.

Wings fluttered within his stomach, the discomfort spread throughout the rest of him. "And, um, what might that be?"

Lillian's small hand clasped his, and she pulled him along as she ran towards the doors.

Oh no.

She pushed through the large arched doors, dragging a stumbling Chance behind, he had to duck to pass through the exit.

The orange glow of midday sun reflected off the sands and stones of the guild grounds.

"What are you doing Lillian? You're going the wrong way. The guild lies outside the city of Pollenton, it's an hour's walk to it, then a carriage ride from there. You're heading towards the mountains."

"I'm heading towards the gardens I saw when I first came here," she said, bouncing with glee.

"Why?"

"I'll show you, stop complaining."

He followed Lillian as she led him around the guild grounds. The walk consisted of much grumbling on his part, as well as moping. After all, there was much to mope over. A carpet of every vibrant color imaginable, came into view. The guild gardens.

Petals blanketed the ground ahead, some taking flight under the gentle gusts of wind that brushed past the pair every so often. Lillian leapt, sending her hand into a wide arc through the air. She landed smiling.

Chance stepped closer, leaning over. "What is it?"

She opened her hand, a white blossom sat upon her palm. Somehow it remained undisturbed by the wind rustling their hair and clothes. Lillian brought the flower to her lips. Her smile widened before she mouthed something Chance could not make out. The petals twitched, but there was no rush of wind to stir them.

Chance bent at the waist. He brought himself as close as possible to the flower, his nose almost brushing Lillian's hand. It shuddered upon Lillian's palm. A moment later, and it began to dance, rocking, spinning, and nearly leap from her hand all together. The petals shrunk, tightening as lines creased their surface. Soon they withered and fell, leaving only the core of the flower. That too, was possessed by same force that compelled the whole flower to jump before.

"What's happening?"

Lillian ignored him, whispering to the plant once more. It ceased its movements for a second. Then the piece shivered like a child caught in the cold, something began to protrude from all its sides. Petals of bright orange, red, and yellow, unfurled from the center, fanning out around it. The new flower bloomed and inched its way up from her hand as a slender green stem grew from beneath. The stem coiled like a thin snake, winding upon itself to sit neatly in her hand.

"You're a Green-leaf," Chance breathed in a near whisper.

She nodded, still smiling.

A powerful one.

"For you, Chance. Thank you for what you did back in the Guild. Standing up for me." Lillian pushed the flower towards him.

"Oh no," he said, raising a hand to protest. "I'm allergic."

She persisted, pushing the flower closer. "You won't be, I promise. Smell."

Chance plucked the flower from her grasp, shutting his eyes as he brought it to his nose. He inhaled. Chance's eyes shot open as a bouquet of citrus filled his senses, the smell almost tangible. He breathed through his mouth and could almost feel the sour notes of lemon roll over his tongue. The sweetness of oranges followed.

"Thank you Lillian." He tucked the flower inside his coat, smoothing the pocket over a few times with his hand as he did. "Now come on, we still have to find a way to Thistle town, unless you prefer to walk?"

Lillian didn't meet his eyes for a moment. Instead she stared at the ground, grinding one foot back and forth into a patch of grass. "There was another reason I brought you here."

Chance arched an eyebrow. "Oh?"

Without a word, Lillian sprinted off.

He exhaled a breath of frustration and set after her. The grass grew longer the further he raced into the gardens, brushing his knees as he drew closer to Lillian. She stopped at the base of a tree. Its bark was the color of iron long gone to rust. The tree loomed over the far side of the guild and, at certain times of the day, its shadow would cover a large bit of the gardens. Every branch bore leaves the color of sapphires, a rich and deep blue. Chance had never seen another tree like it.

"Why did you bring me to the Guild tree?"

"I have a faster way to get to Thistle town. Come on," she beckoned with a hand as she began climbing the tree.

"Oh no, that's a bad idea! People fall from trees, that's how they get hurt. Lillian!"

She continued climbing.

Chance grumbled to himself and followed. He slipped his staff through a wide loop on the side of his coat and threw his arms tight around what bit of the trunk he managed to grab. "Children," he muttered. "Reckless. Never listen. Stubborn. Crazy. Bad luck."

Lillian sat atop the nearest branch, it was thicker than Chance was, holding her weight with ease. She waved at him, cheery smile still plastered to her face.

Chance mouthed his discontent in silence, making all manner of unpleasant faces as he scrambled over to her. "Why are we sitting on a tree, the Guild's most respected tree nonetheless?"

"I'm showing you a faster way to travel!"

He blinked. "Um, Lillian, I feel that I should share with you that trees are not known for being quick...or moving at all."

"That is because most people do not know how to properly motivate a tree."

106

"What?"

"Hold on tight," she advised.

"Hold on to what?"

Lillian pressed herself against the branch, straddling it with all her limbs. Bowing her head close to the bark, she whispered, and the tree shook.

Chance threw himself at the branch, wrapping himself around it. His stomach knotted and it felt like his legs had become bits of rope. He shut his eyes. Something moved within his grasp and he yelped.

The branch was moving. It slithered forwards, carrying the both of them along with it. Wind rushed over his face as the branch picked up speed. The air flowing past them increased as the branch darted through the sky.

"You should close your eyes," advised Lillian. "Oh, and your mouth. Bugs do not taste good!"

Chance obliged, shutting eyes and mouth. It was a pity he couldn't turn off his brain. *I'm going to die in a tree. Or I'm going to fall and die hitting the ground. I'm going to die. I hate children. I hate people. I hate quests! I hate trees!*

The world beneath him continued to rush forwards, his stomach felt like it had somersaulted several times over, and bile crept up the back of Chance's throat. *Let it end. Magic be merciful, let it end.*

Everything slowed. Harsh wind ceased to buffet Chance's eyelids, and his hair was no longer being whipped around. "Oh good," he breathed. "I'm dead."

"No, we're here."

Chance opened his eyes. He regretted it the moment he did, it was a long way down. "Where are we?"

"In the air, outside the walls of Thistle town."

"That...that's impossible. The distance... how fast were we going, Lillian?"

"Fast enough," she smiled. "And my father told me that one ought not to use the word 'impossible'. Not in this world, not when concerning things like wizards, and especially magic."

Chance grunted in agreement. "How do we get down?"

"With these," Lillian held a fistful of vines, each thicker than Chance's thumb.

"Where did those come from?"

"I grew them on the ride over here," Lillian wound several lengths of vines around her waist. She twined five separate strands together, throwing them over the branch and securing them with several knots. Scooting over until she was beside Chance, she shot him an inquiring look. "Well?"

He sighed, following her example. "Now what?" he tugged on his knot, unsure of its integrity.

"Have you ever fallen from a tree before?"

"No...I don't make a habit of it."

"Oh," she looked down at her knees for a moment. "This isn't going to be fun for you."

"What isn't—" Lillian's hand pressed against his chest. She pushed. Chance tumbled off the branch, and before he could scream, the vines constricted around his midsection. The back of his legs were brushing against the branch. "Are we stuck?"

"No," she ran one of her hands across the vines. They lengthened.

Chance felt his body sink lower, inch by inch, they grew further from the tree. He squirmed, working to right himself. "This isn't as bad as I thought it would be."

"It's a bit of a trip down Chance, can I ask you about your magic now?"

Exhaling, he ran his tongue around the back of his teeth, thinking of where to begin. "Do you know why my last name is Fortunes?"

"No?" she shook her head.

"I come from a long line of wizards who have the peculiar ability to affect luck—fortune, we can create it and alter it upon will. For as long anyone can remember, wizards in my family brought about good luck. Change the odds in battle. Turn horrible circumstances into favorable ones. Literally bring and shift fortunes. Eventually the name stuck. My family lost their old one, and became the Fortunes.

"I'm the first, and only wizard," he broke off, swallowing for a moment. "To be born with the powers of misfortune. Everywhere I go, my power acts out, I don't have the best of control with it. Bad things happen. Sometimes, terrible things happen. And on occasion, worse things happen."

Lillian bowed her head. "I'm sorry, Chance."

"It's okay, I've gotten rather—"

Memories of an unpleasant nature flooded his mind upon seeing the imposing structure of stone. It was a shade of red long since faded by time and the elements, bleached into something brighter by the sun.

"What happened there?" Lillian jabbed a finger at the wall.

A lump formed in his throat. Chance swallowed, but the air refused to go down. He prayed that the descent would increase in speed and take them away from the sight. A section large enough to be a small home was missing from the pinkish wall. The edges that remained were rough, unattended to, and deteriorating. "I happened. Well, my magic did."

"Oh..." Lillian turned her head, adopting silence.

Chance exhaled slowly through his nose. Things would get complicated soon, the people of Thistle town would not be happy to see him again. The vines lowered them to the point where he could see the ground, and the entrance to the town, which was bustling with people about their business. His fingers trailed over the rough surface of his staff, and he muttered to himself about hoping to go about their quest unnoticed.

Firm ground met his feet and pushed against him with considerable force. Chance bent at the waist, running his hands over his knees and shins. "I'm too old for this."

"Come on!" Lillian undid her harness, and sped off towards the town gates.

He clawed at the vines. They resisted, stretching, knotting themselves further, and almost at times, tightening further. "Magic be merciful!" he spat, sending the point of his boot crashing into the dirt. A clod of earth sailed into the air and struck a passerby on the chest.

They stopped.

Chance freed himself from his entanglement and mumbled an apology before turning to following Lillian.

"Chance Fortunes?" they said.

The notion to ignore the person, and run, was rather tempting. Instead, he answered. "Yes?"

Apparently it was the wrong thing to do. The man spun on heel, shouting as he took off down the road in the other direction. All eyes turned to him.

In all the years of people eyeing him, it was just as uncomfortable now as it had been when they first started.

Every other person in the immediate vicinity began taking step back. Some went as far as to avert their eyes. Seems like the smart thing to do. Chance followed their example and turned his gaze away. "Right then, nice to meet you all, lovely town, good bye!" he walked after Lillian, making sure to take long strides to carry him all the quicker away from the gathering folk.

The sound of footsteps that were not his, prompted him to cast a glance over his shoulder. Many of townspeople were following him to the gate. He quickened his pace, slipped his staff from the loop, and then broke into a run. The townspeople set chase.

"I haven't done anything yet!"

He pumped his legs harder, Chance had been running all his life from danger and into trouble, they were not going to catch him. A group of folk up ahead, formed a tight knit group, one that blocked his progress.

"Stop!" the group shouted in unison.

Chance did not oblige, refusing to slow.

"Please!"

He skidded to a halt, his knees taking the brut of the force, causing him to fight from toppling over.

A rather plump woman, dressed in purple, stepped out from the group. She reminded him of a plum. Her cheeks were padded with a hint of extra flesh, but it gave the woman a warm, and motherly look.

"Please, Chance, turn away. Go back to the Guild. We don't want anymore trouble." She reached into the folds of her clothing and removed a fist sized sack. With a flick of her wrist, she sent it tumbling through the air.

Chance fumbled as he cupped his hands together. The sack jingled upon landing, and with it, Chance's heart sank. He knew what they were doing.

"I'm sorry. I'm not here by will, I'm here as a Guild guide, new member, and... the Guild Master might have wanted me to take some time away from the Guild. I can't take your money though." He tossed the bag back.

The woman made no motion to catch it, letting it fall to the ground.

"Whatever quest it is, we'll pay you to turn and leave. Please, Chance, the last time you were here—the damage— we could hardly pay to fix that."

Rocks settled into his stomach, weighing him down, but he did not budge. "People are missing," he said, his voice low but the words cutting through the air with effect.

The gathered people exchanged sullen looks. "We'll hire someone else from the guild, and still pay you. Please leave Chance."

Blonde hair caught his eye. Lillian's head bobbed into view as she jumped to get a better view from behind the crowd.

"No."

"No?"

"No," Chance repeated, his voice iron. *I hate this, I hate quests, but I'm not going to let her down on her first one.*

He stepped forward, bending to retrieve the fallen sack, and pressed it into the woman's hands. "I'll find those people, and I promise, no damage."

The plump woman blinked. She bowed her head in understanding. "Alright, move!" she shooed the crowd away with a raised hand. "Shoo!"

They dispersed and Chance found himself wishing he could muster such power in his hand.

"Chance," she sighed, "you're a good boy. Find our folk, do right, and don't... don't for love of tiny turtles—"

"You don't actually believe in that, do you ma'am? That there is an ocean of tiny turtles, on the backs of which are the lands of the world?"

She snapped her wrist.

"Ow," Chances hands flew to his nose, groping the spot where her fingers had struck.

The rotund plum-like woman waggled her forefinger in admonishment. "Don't you cast doubt on things you know nothing about Chance. Finish your quest, don't muck about, and don't destroy my town! You hear?"

Chance bobbed his head.

"Good," she thrust her chest forward and released a, "harrumph." With that, she turned and left Chance alone with the remaining member from the crowd.

Lillian stood a few feet from Chance. "What was all that about?"

"How much did you see?"

"Most of it."

He let out a breath, walking over to her and placed a hand on her shoulder. "I'll tell you as we walk. Come on."

Chance gave her a gentle push as he took the lead, wandering past the gates in search of someone more amenable to speaking with him.

"That's how I make a great deal of my money," he said.

Lillian did not respond.

"Townspeople know of my reputation. It's spread quite a bit," his posture sunk. "Many of them pay me to leave, not get involved whatsoever, and then request another guild member."

"That's horrible Chance, I'm sorry."

He shrugged, "It's okay, I'm used to it. I don't like taking their money, but at times... they don't leave me much choice. But I've made a small fortune that way."

Lillian sucked her lower lip between her teeth, and fiddled with her fingers. "Have you ever..." she trailed off.

"What?"

"Finished a quest? Completely?" she threw her hands over her mouth as she finished speaking, regretting the words.

His body shook from the laughter. "Yes, I have."

"You're not mad?"

"No Lillian, I expected that remark. I've finished my fair share of quests but that's not to say they didn't have their unpleasant moments." Chance hooked a thumb to the hole in the town wall.

Her eyes fixated on the wall for a moment. Turning back to Chance, she mouthed the word, "Ah."

Every few steps, someone would turn their head to glance at the pair. Some went as far at to gawk at Chance. Lillian flashed them a weak smile, hoping to placate the townsfolk.

It didn't work.

She reached out and pinched the sleeve of his leather coat, tugging on it to get his attention.

Chance turned his head. "Hm?"

"What now? We're here, how do we find who or what took the people?"

"We ask."

"That's it, it's that simple?"

Chance nodded. "More often than not, the greatest mysteries are, in my experience, rather simple. We overcomplicate them."

"Maybe it's like that with your magic, Chance."

A sharp jolt went through his ankle and the world slipped. Chance jabbed the ground with the butt of his staff, using it to prevent him from falling completely. He blinked several time, absorbing what Lillian had suggested.

"Chance?" said Lillian.

Overcomplicating my own magic?

"Chance? Chance!"

The reverie slipped, and Chance saw why Lillian was calling for his attention. The boy came up to his collar, tall for his age, unkempt black hair that had spent some time in the dirt. He had an unremarkable ruddy face, which like the hair, and his clothes in fact, were close friends with grime.

"Oh, hello, you...there. Person."

The boy ran a finger below his nose several times, blinking as he did.

Chance titled his head towards his companion. "Lillian?"

She placed a hand on the boy's arm, gently nudging him towards Chance. "He says he knows something about the missing folk."

"Oh? That's wonderful. Not that the people are missing, that's terrible of course. Er, what exactly does he know?"

"Go on," Lillian urged the boy.

The boy inhaled, his nose sniffling and shaking as he did. Chance winced at the grating sound. "People been talkin' and I heard things..." the boy trailed off, looking to Chance.

When it was clear Chance didn't understand why, he sighed, extending a free hand.

Lillian reached out, cupping the boy's hands with her own. "It's okay, tell him."

"He wants money, Lillian."

Her face contorted, eyes narrowing dangerously. "You want money, for us to help you find your own townsfolk? You should be ashamed!" Lillian's fingers twitched and the girl looked to be on the verge of slapping the boy.

Chance took a step back as the young woman gave the boy a tongue lashing that would leave the boy feeling scoured raw. "It's okay, Lillian," Chance stepped forward, offering a calming hand. She turned to glare at him, her body heaving from the shouting.

"Tell him!" she snapped.

The boy's body went rigid and he rattled off every bit of information he knew. "Heard folks mentioning them apes is 'sponsible. Them things been poking 'round the edges of town, taking small animals. Heard 'em took calves first, some dogs, even a few children," the boy's body shook as he mentioned the last bit. "Anyone with no wall ta hide behind had chance to got took."

"Apes..." Chance said. "Hairy things, made to look like silly little people?"

The boy shook his head. "Don't know what apes you've seen. These things are tall, taller than you. No hair—scales, like lizards. Heard 'em got forked tongues, and wings."

"Wings?" Chance and Lillian said in unison.

"I said so, didn't I?" the boy puffed his chest, taking offense at their doubt. He raised his arms to his side, flapping them as he mimed a pair of wings. "Them like to wears hats too, small ones."

Chance's teeth rode over one another as they ground. He was used to being mocked—it was nothing new. But to be mocked by a child, one making light of the fact people were missing...it did not sit well with him.

Fingers tightening around his staff, he stepped forward, his figure blocking the sun and casting the boy in his shadow. Chance bent at the waist, looming over the child.

With a flourish, he spun his staff and placed it against the boy's chest. "Do you know what I am, boy? I'm wizard. A terrible one!"

It wasn't a lie as far as he was concerned; Guild Master Pui-pui said as much. "Lying to a wizard is a terrible thing, we sort can turn you into any number of horrible creatures...like frogs. Ever been a frog before?"

If the boy shook his head any faster, Chance worried the child's vision would be left permanently spinning.

"No?" A thin, wry smile spread over his face. "We should fix that." Chance accentuated the statement with a prod of his staff.

The boy's lips quivered and sweat beaded on his face. "Not lying, sir...wizard...wizard-sir. Please, don't make me a frog. I've seen 'em, dogs 'round here chase 'em, and..." the boy swallowed. "And eat 'em."

Chance's smile grew wider. "That's right, they do," he cackled maniacally.

Passersby stopped, turning to glance at the laughing wizard. When Chance directed his gaze towards them, they scattered, leaving the path empty save for Lillian, the boy, and himself.

"What kind of frog would you like to be?" Chance leaned closer, stretching his smile to the point that his cheeks and lips ached.

"Caves!" the boy shouted, his voice taking a shrill turn. "Heard me ma cursing 'bout some caves."

"Where?"

The boy jabbed a finger towards a meadow lying on the outskirt of the town. "Not more than an hours walk past that. Please sir, I ain't wanting to be a frog. Please," the boy clapped his hands together, pleading.

"Lillian and I will be back to let you know what sort of frog you'll be, if we come back without the people of this town. If we find them...then maybe I shan't make you into dog food."

"Tiny turtles be blessed, thank you!" The boy backpedaled several feet, spinning on the point of one foot before running at a speed Chance found impressive, and he himself was an expert in running away.

Following the boy's excellent example, Chance left the scene, aiming to leave the town behind.

Lillian fell in step, walking a few inches apart. "Well, that was rather frightening."

"You think so?"

"Frightened me."

"Oh god," Chance panted, relieved. "For a moment, I thought I was the only one. Being scary is...well scary."

"Would you have really done it?"

"I had half a mind to, at least when I thought he was lying."

"Could you have done it?"

"Hm? I don't know, Lillian," Chance leaned closer, looming over her as he did with the boy. A lopsided grin slid over his face. "We should find out."

"Stop it," she said, lashing out with her hand.

Chance frowned, rubbing his arm. "That was rude."

"So was scaring me."

"Sorry," he mumbled. "It's new for me, I rather like it. It's safer than actually fighting. The best battle is the one that never happens, I always say. Or the one you can walk away from without a scratch. Either or, really."

"So what now, Chance?"

"We walk to the cave," he said with a booming laugh.

"Could you make it not sound so terrifying."

"Sorry," his voice dropped to a whisper, "we walk to the cave."

"Thank you, Chance."

"In which there dwell horrible scaled, winged fiends, that snatch children and small animals, creatures with a penchant for...hats!"

Lillian sighed.

"Nothing wrong with a bit of story to pass the time as we walk, we have about an hour."

"There's a bit of story, and then there is, well whatever that was."

They crossed into the meadow, bickering lightheartedly as they walked. When they ran out of things to speak about, they progressed in silence, Chance's eyes darting around the field as the sunlight faded. An hour passed.

Chance had never once seen a whale before, terrifying creatures from what he'd read. Obscenely large, with cavernous mouths that could swallow things whole. He imagined that the entrance to the cave was very much like the mouth of a whale from the stories, if of course they were made of stone...and had teeth. Jagged protrusions crept out from the stony maw, reaching down, giving the impression that wouldn't be entering the cavern, but being eaten.

"Wizards do not get frightened," Chance murmured. "Wizards are stoic, wise, and terrifying, they do not get frightened. Wizards do the frightening."

"What was that?"

"Nothing," he answered, gripping his staff tighter as he straightened his posture. Chance steeled himself and slid between the rocky fangs hanging from the opening. His eyes tightened, fighting to make out the path ahead in the darkness.

"We should've brought a torch," said Lillian.

Chance brought his staff to his lips. "I can make a small fire."

Lillian's hand shot out in the dark, grabbing Chance's staff, pulling it away from his mouth. "Maybe you should let me try?" she suggested. Brushing her hands over the cold, porous stone, she reached out with her senses. It was difficult picking up on it, but the faint throb of plant life was there. A gentle humming sensation vibrated against her skin.

Placing her tongue between her teeth, she focused, calling out to the buried plants, and pulled. Stone shuddered, minute cracks rang around them, rock protested and then gave way to whip like tendrils that crawled out from the world below.

Something flickered in the dark, like the first rays of morning sun creeping over the horizon, only to be blotted out by a group of towering trees. Bulbs no larger than his thumb, sat on the end of every hair like plant that stretched around them. As they vibrated against the cavern walls, Chance noticed a dim glow emanating within the buds. It wasn't the pale bright luminescence from stories, that would illuminate all darkness, blinding the ill things that inhabited said dark. The light was something warmer, gentler, like a late autumn evening's sun, an orange-tinged golden hue.

"Wow," he breathed, "impressive. I was going to light the top of my staff on fire. This is better."

"Thank you," Lillian beamed, her teeth gleamed and her skin shone bronze under the lights glow.

Chance nodded and led as they moved their way through the cave. He frowned when his foot sank further than expected, leaving his ankle cold, and his sock clinging to his skin with a great deal of moisture.

"Of course there are puddles in here," he grumbled.

A high pitched shriek carried through the cave, rattling loose sediment from the wall above. Dust speckled their clothes and Chance felt various parts of his body tighten in response to the sudden scream. Seconds later, more followed behind, too varied in timing and voice to be echoes.

"There's more than one, whatever they are," he reasoned.

"I told you not to scare me, Chance."

"It's okay, Lillian."

"It is?"

"Yes, I'm scared too."

"That doesn't help me..."

Another scream. "Help!" Something in the voice galvanized Chance, pulling on a part of him that helped bury his fear.

"We're here to help them, not be helped. We're wizards, Lillian, we do the rescuing, the helping, and the scaring!" A maniacal smile spread over his face as he finished, made all the more fearsome by the lighting cast by the plants.

Lillian took several cautioned steps back.

"Come on Lillian, there are people to save. Monsters to scare, magic and mayhem ahead!" He released a shrill cry of his own and stormed forwards, holding his staff high so it rattled against the cave ceiling. A chilling clacking sound echoed as he ran ahead.

Lillian sighed, "There is something very wrong with that man. Wait for me!"

She ran after him.

Chance burst into a clearing, still hollering at the top of his lungs, staff being pumped into the air like a madman. His cries died out when he realized the opening was absent the light from Lillian's plants. Chance rested his staff against his forehead as he narrowed his eyes, peering ahead. A chorus of cackling rang out, and it wasn't coming from him. His hackles rose as whistling filled the air.

He was left a second to drop to the floor in order to avoid its source. Whatever it had been crashed into the stone behind, shattering. The ground pricked, and scraped against his legs and the soft flesh of his palms as he crawled. Fingering the smooth, white substance that had clattered against the wall, he realized it was shale. He slid his finger across a larger piece that hadn't been reduced to chips, and brushed across a piece of fabric.

The lining of his throat seared as bile crept up. It wasn't shale. It was bone.

Whatever frenzied courage that had bubbled up inside him, had died.

Oh no, oh no, this is bad!

Lillian came screaming into the room, mimicking his crazed screams. "Fear us, for we are wizards, and we will make you into frogs!" Her screams were silenced as her plants followed her in, shining light on Chance and what was in his hands. She threw her hands over her mouth.

Light filled the room, Lillian's plants wound their way up the stone walls and across the floor. A stone pillar jutted out from the ground, near the center of the room. It was rough, and yet not as jagged as the stone comprising the rest of the cave. It bore innumerous marks and indentations. That wasn't what held the attention of the newest guild member and her guide.

Crude bindings made from tattered clothing, what looked to be long lengths of matted hair, and vines, held a group of people against the pillar.

"The missing townsfolk," Chance's voice came out like the coarse stone around him.

The light brought into view more than the missing people, such as the things that took them. For as long as he lived Chance had considered himself tall, correcting people's assumptions of what the word truly meant even among those that thought to embody the word themselves.

Now he stood corrected.

If Lillian stood upon his shoulders, then maybe she would be able to land a solid punch to the creature's sternum. The closest of the creature's limbs looked too long and ill proportioned, like someone had stretched them to the point of ridiculousness. Their bodies were covered in mottled scales of earthen-brown and moss-greens, placed over mounds of stringy muscle. When they smiled at the pair, it reminded Chance of his promise to turn the boy into a frog. A promise Chance reminded himself not to fulfill.

The boy had not lied about the wings, which were not the bird like limbs he envisioned. It was as if giant bats had nestled themselves into the backs of the scaly apes. The boy did not lie about the hats either...

Chance blinked, working to clear his vision as he noticed each monster donned a small cap resembling an upturned cup. Tiny Turtles, why would they need or want those? One of the monsters snapped him out of his thoughts as it marched towards him, wearing what looked to be several dresses haphazardly stitched together to create a mess.

"Looks like they sent us more," the creature rumbled, its voice shaking loose stone from its foundations.

What does he mean by that?

"Are you...wearing a dress?"

"Lillian," Chance hissed. "One should not criticize the fashion choices of monsters. Especially those taller, and scarier than me."

The winged, scaly ape, opened its mouth, every one of its needle like teeth glistened in the new cave lighting. "It's slimming," it said.

"And quite so, if I must say so myself, and I do, I do." Chance said, doubling over and making his posture the least threatening he could. "My friend and I seem to be lost, if you'll excuse us, you know how these caves are, they all look the same, monsters in each and every one, hehe. Wrong monsters, wrong quest, the princess we're looking for must be in another cavern. We'll go now."

The creature's face twisted, and its ridged brows knitted together. A forked tongue slipped out from between its teeth, sliding over its lips, which soon spread back into the froglike smile from earlier. "Which one?"

Chance's mouth twitched for a moment. "I'm sorry?"

"Which one goes, which one stays?" There was a sickening gleam in the monsters eyes when it posed the question.

"Well seeing how it was both of us who wandered in here by quite the accident, it will be said both of us, who will in fact be leaving." Chance gave the beasts a quick wave of his hand, spun on heel and marched. "Take care," he called over his shoulder.

"No," the single word rolled through the cavern with authority. "They promised us one more. Which one?"

Chance stopped. He turned to face the monsters, keeping an eye trained on them, and one on the blonde figure skulking behind the rocky formations on the cave floor. "Who promised you what?"

The ape placed a thick hand to the side of its head, scratching the area around its diminutive cap. "Folk from the town."

It might as well have sank one of its shovel sized fists into Chance's stomach, than say that—it would have elicited the same effect. Chance pressed a hand to his body, trying to quell the troubling sensation. "And...what did they promise you?"

Slender, barb-like teeth filled Chance's view as the creature leaned forward, smacking its lips. "Food."

The monster crooked a finger in the direction of Chance. "Townsfolk got fed up with us taking people on whim, when we could, however many we could. Struck a deal. They'd send us some, no fuss—"

One of the prisoners bound to the pillar screamed. Another of the creatures silenced it with a slap that rang throughout the space.

The talkative ape leered, "Well, maybe a little fuss. Spicy ones taste better." It punctuated the statement with another smack of its lips. "S'boring this way though, was much more fun taking 'em wriggling, screaming, and fighting. But, easier is nice too."

The muscles in Chance's hand ached. His fingers quivered as he held them against his staff tight enough to cause the wood to creak. Muscles along his jaw begged for reprieve as they remained locked, his teeth grinding upon one another.

"So which one? You, or the girl?" The creature broke away, turning his head to face the rock Lillian was creeping behind. Its nostrils flared and it inhaled in several short bursts.

Chance's body shook, the amount of blood rushing to his face caused the entirety of head to throb in rhythm with his escalating heart rate.

"Can't decide?" The creature took a step towards the rock Lillian hid behind.

She darted behind another, maneuvering her way closer to the pillar with the towns folk.

The creature's head tracked her as she did. "I can smell you, girl." It turned back to Chance. "If you don't choose, maybe I will. The girl then? She looks—"

"Quiet!" the air cracked when Chance spoke.

The remainder of the monsters joined their loud mouthed brethren, taking up positions on either side. They scowled in unison, baring their teeth, their hands cracking as they made fists. One of the bunch decided it a good idea to rush towards the spot where Lillian hid.

Chance Fortunes lost control. A primal and incoherent scream left his lungs, filling the area. He thrust his staff towards the air, a lance of pure force erupted from it, jarring the joints in his arm. As the wooden tool bucked, its magical discharge struck the ceiling, ricocheting around the cave with the sound of thunder.

Nothing further happened.

Chance blinked. "Erhm..."

The masks of horror that was on the creature's faces, slipped, replaced by ever widening smiles. "Get him," ordered the leader of the winged apes. A chorus of hoots, shrills and shrieks erupted. Several of the monsters reached behind themselves, filling their hands with a substances apes were notorious for using as a projectile. The situation escalated with the clumps of excrement ignited within their hands.

"Oh..."

With a deafening roar, the apes hurled their flaming fecal matter towards him.

"No! No, no, no!" Chance flailed his arms, waving his staff in all manner of frantic patterns.

The world shook. Thunder filled his ears and stone fell from above. Every piece of fiery waste that was hurtling towards him, struck a piece of falling stone.

As the ground quaked, one of the creature's lost its balance, the bit of incendiary poo it was holding, slipped. It howled as the fecal matter clung to its scales, setting it afire.

Chance's teeth rattled within his skull, clacking against one another as everything continued to shake. More fire streaked through the air, and Chance did what any wizard of his caliber would do.

He ran.

"I am not dying like this!" he bobbed, avoiding a particularly impressive sized fireball that impacted the wall ahead, splattering and spreading its noxious flames across the wall. "Haha, serves you right!" Chance hooted in triumph, jabbing his staff towards the fire engulfed ape.

Bat-like screeches came from the remaining fiends as they took the air.

"Oh, oh no."

They swerved their way around the stone that rained down, setting after him with simpler implements. Claws and fangs.

Chance swatted one across the mouth with his staff, it was a fleshy impact, splitting the beast's lips, and sending a few of its teeth free from its mouth. Another creature held its arms over its head, fingers intertwined. He scampered to the side as the monster brought its fists down. Stone shattered. Twisting his hips, he slashed through the air with his staff, striking the back of the ape's legs. It staggered, swaying before the inevitable. Oh no. Clawing at the ground, Chance pulled himself from the spot where the monster collapsed into a crumpled heap.

The cave shuddered and more stone fell. It sounded like a rotten fruit falling to the ground as it landed upon the recently toppled ape. Its friends roared in protest, circling Chance.

He swallowed and shut his eyes.

The ground cracked, vines bursting forth and into the air. They wrapped their way around the creatures, hauling them back to the cavern floor.

"Run, Chance!" Lillian shouted from her position at that pillar. She tore at the bindings, working to free the missing people.

Chance steeled himself, running past the strung up apes, the falling debris and flaming poo that stuck to the stone around him. Making it to the pillar, he set to work aiding Lillian in freeing the people. Chance sunk his teeth into the cloth holding the people. Salt and dirt filled his mouth, "Ackh," he spat, recoiling. Wedging his staff between the bonds, he pried as Lillian continued tug and tear. The bindings gave way.

Lillian knelt, extending a hand to help haul a child to her feet.

Chance pointed to the exit, "Go!" He raced ahead of the group. *Over complicating my own magic, hm?*

Chance twisted his body, skidding to a halt. The apes were still suspended within Lillian's vines. He cackled. "I am Chance Fortunes! Wizard, conjurer of magic, bringer of mayhem, slayer of monsters most foul!" His cackling grew louder, overtaking all other sound, along with his sanity for the moment. "Ehyeooow!" He screamed, waving his staff. Magic built inside him, coursing through staff, blasting out its end. It erupted like a wave breaking on the shore, spilling throughout the entirety of the cavern.

Lillian's vines turned to dust. The creatures were freed. And from above, it sounded as if the world had cracked in half. Stone split like frayed cloth, and with it, all but one of the apes were struck by the falling earth.

"Run!" Chance bellowed, gesturing to the freed people. He watched as Lillian led them, somehow managing to avoid being hit by anything larger than stones the size of fingernails. Chance dallied behind, watching for any stragglers or the rogue ape.

A piercing cry wracked his ears. The final ape soared towards him. Chance turned, now standing within the exit of the cave. Holding his staff up high, he released a cry of his own. "You shall not pass!" he slammed his staff into the ground, channeling his magic into the floor below.

Nothing happened. The beast grew closer, shrieking in fury.

"You...should not pass!" Chance struck the ground again.

No effect.

"Do...do not pass." Chance struck for the third and final time. And bad luck came in threes.

A stone a bit smaller than his own head, struck the ape in its back, causing it to falter. The monster impacted the ground with enough force to crush the stone beneath it. Its scales were ripped from its body as it slid forward. Bad luck made its second stroke. A series of rocks in varying sizes fell upon the fiend's leg, crushing the limb and leaving it pinned.

The stone above Chance's head shivered, and he stepped back, prodding the rock with his staff. Gazing down at the monster, he smiled.

"I am the Wizard of Misfortune."

Bad luck struck thrice, the roof collapsed, trapping the creature within the deteriorating cavern. Chance cackled as he ran, the laughter growing to the point of being uncontrollable. Rocks continued to fall behind him. He pushed his legs harder, ignoring the burning within them.

The mouth of the cave was up ahead. Chance pushed harder, racing out of the cave and into the meadows as the last of the stone fell. The cave had collapsed in full.

He placed his hands on his knees, panting. His lungs felt full of sand, irritated and dry. Chance's throat was raw and his heart throbbed to the point where he felt it throughout his entire body. He straightened himself, looked to the sky and laughed. "We did it. We did it—oomph!" he fell back as Lillian crashed into him, throwing her weight against his body. Chance blinked several times, fighting to remember how to breathe and regain the air she had knocked from his lungs.

"We did it!" she cheered.

"We did it," he coughed in agreement.

With his palms pressed against her shoulders, Chance eased Lillian off him. Rising to his feet, he surveyed the townsfolk. They were grim stained, haggard, malnourished—tired. Worst of all—betrayed. Chance felt a hint of the madness and anger from before, resurging. "Your own neighbors, friends, families, gave you away to those things?"

The folk avoided his gaze, nodding in silence as an answer.

"I can't believe it!" Lillian snarled. "Tiny turtles be blessed, how could they? What are we going to do, Chance?"

Chance gripped his staff, feeling for the first time, his magic under control. He smiled. "I think, Lillian, that Thistle town should be paid a visit by the Wizard of Misfortune. A wall could do with another hole. There will be reckoning on account of these folk. Maybe, a series of unfortunate events will befall some of the people responsible."

"And maybe turn a few people into frogs, Chance?"

"And maybe turn a few people into frogs," he cackled.

Cuhlyn's Tale - The Crossroad

Joshua Cejka

Rat held his porous cloak over his head and watched Finger stuff his fat sodden face with the last of the mutton. The cloak wasn't doing much. It never had, but now it was creating a trough right over his head which spouted a steady waterfall right in front of his face and into his disintegrating boots, festering his puckered toes inside their woolen stockings. Finger - so named because he'd once knocked out a small farmer with one thump of his huge finger - didn't seem to mind the rain. You could see the huge fat drops smash against his fat bald head with such force that a little misty halo of exploded droplets ringed around him. He dropped his elephantine rear on a fallen tree on the other side of the crossroads. The force of him sitting travelled through the ground and up the stump Rat was sitting on, jarring him.

"Lookit that fat bastard."

"Eats like a king he does," Scab agreed from his own makeshift shelter, cobbled together with a lattice of bare branches and held like a sultans shade over his own head.

"Remind me again why we keep him around?" Rat itched for a smoke but the rain wouldn't let up. For the eightieth time that morning he dragged his gaze around the hazy dark sentries of the forest for any little place that might afford shelter from the downpour to light one up, but there was nothing. What little leaves there were clinging like quivering children to late autumn branches as a steady cold wind dragged down from the mountain passes with desperate claws. Most of them had given up and settled into a thick mat of sodden crap all over everything.

"Ee's my sister's cousin. And he's big and scary looking."

"If'n the eedjits only knew he had the temper of a big fluffy bunny.."

"Aye. And the grace of a drunk ogre with a belly full of beans."

Coal sloshed into the frame made by the waterfall cloak and glanced over at the big man, now tossing the bone from his mutton over his shoulder.

"I don't know, Rat, my friend. There was that scrap at The Smoking Pig. He was pretty good in that."

Rat peered around the waterfall at Coal. The slight adjustment altered the course of the river such that it ran straight down his sleeve and over his formerly dry chest, chilling his heart. Coal was smoking, he could see. He was cupping a hand over the bowl of his pipe, protecting it from the downpour. It was producing a pretty nice smoke. He also noticed that Coal seemed, of the five of them, the driest and most cheerful which only made him want to stab him more. All the young gals back at the home place - who couldn't endure his grin with any sense of personal propriety - loaded him up with treated gum blankets and warm cloaks and liners. Compared to the rest of them, he looked like a dandy. A dry and happy dandy.

"Gimme a piece of that pipe, Coal."

Coal immediately tucked it into his chest, his well-wrapped hand still cupped over the smoldering bowl. A simpering hurt look washed over the rakish dandy's dripping face. Rat hated that look. It kindled something mean in the bleak pit of his heart and made him want to punch it in, but Coal was his nephew and he'd never hear the end of it. Apparently, his wife was not immune to the boy's charm either.

"Ain't my fault you never switched to pipe, Rat, my man. Bet you don't have such as a scrap of dry leaf left to you." Coal took a draw from the pipe to emphasize his point.

"All the more reason to pinch yours. Gimme some."

"Darby portioned it out fairly. Ain't my fault you cain't smoke your'n. Next time we hit the Pig you buy yerself a pipe off my man Forsmyth. You'll thank me."

Rat sneered up at him and spit a little stream of stinking rainwater out of his mouth.

"I'll thank ye now if'n you hand it over 'fore I have to beat you for it."

Coal nodded and flashed the rakish smile that all the ladies loved so much, as though he agreed with the sense if not the intent of his friends remark. Coal hadn't yet learned that the charm he radiated only worked with women. In men it boiled their blood. If there was one thing he'd like to personally teach his fancy nephew, it was that.

"Could do that, Rat. Could do. But I'd reckon it'd ruin the pipe and the smoke and then where would we be? All of us smokeless is where. Tell you what. I'll give you a pinch of what's left. You can roll it if you want."

"Paper's are all soaked, you little shit. You know that."

"So they are. So they are. And who's fault is that?"

Scab fidgeted a little to his right on the old log. Rat watched one of his legs kick out at the tendrils of smoke leading off of the remains of last nights fire, testing the ashes for any sign of remaining ember.

"I got me a pipe, Coal. Can I have a pinch?"

"Sure thing Scab, my man. Sure thing. Tell you what though. I'll trade you a pinch for that little bit of sweet you snatched off that brat last week."

"Come on. That was mine fair and fine. You saw the way he bit me for it. And it's all I got left to eat."

"Trade's a trade my man. I'm just trying to be fair about it."

The rain spattering on his cloak tapped out the seconds it took Scab to mull it over in his head during which Coal made a show of smoking his little pipe, selling it even more. In that instant, Rat was certain Coal was stealing from them, maybe even hiding a little straight from the source. He aimed to kill him when he could, wife be damned. It was her fault she had a baseless, untrustworthy shit like that for a nephew. He'd cure her of that sin, even if it added others to her name.

"Alright Coal. You drive a real hard bargain but I'll do it." And with that, Scab's arm reached out with the sugar stick in his hand. He saw Coal reach under his cloak when his hand reappeared it had a good sized handful clenched into his fist. The exchange was made, Coal's grin flashed in the gray light.

"Thanks." He didn't turn to see Scab filling his pipe but he could hear it. "You got a light?"

"Sorry, My man. Sorry. Nothing to light. Maybe if you scratch around in that fire pit you might find a coal or two."

"You could tap out a little of the embers of your own, though. That ought to do it."

"Could do. Could do. But I ain't gonna, my man. Try the pit. It's still smoking a bit. You should find something in there."

"That's just it you skell." Rat dumped the rain off of him and grabbed for his blade. "I've had enough of you. Gonna bleed you right here."

"Awww... Dear me. Whatever will Aunty Shellah say? Well... if we must, dear Uncle, we must." Coal twirled his fancy cloak like he'd must have heard about in some fireside story somewhere. He laid his hand on his own sword. Rat knew it to be a sad bit of steel, ragged and rusty and poorly cared for. Coal was the sort who expected - and usually got - others to do the sharpening on his behalf.

"Y'ain't doing none of that," Darby roared from behind them. It came in like a distant thunder stroke. It was as predictable as Finger's rancid breath. He always stopped any fights among them, and particularly one's that might involve his budding protege, Coal. Where he appeared from, no one could be quite certain. One minute he wasn't there at all, and the next he was, as though the mist and rain just congealed into his ragged cloak filled by his blood scarlet vest.

He'd been a bandit longer and better than any of them. It was said he once scavenged the battlefield of Cathles and that he'd once been an adventurer but the wounds were too much and he quit. At nights when the air was fair and cool, Rat watched him draw Coal aside and draw him into long discussions on the profession of thievery, imparting whatever wisdom he'd stored up.

Long ago, he'd tried the same with Rat when he'd been favorite. But then Rat went and got himself married. That's how he always thought of it, when he thought of it at all. Marriage was something that happened by accident, like stepping into a pile of horse shit. You did your best to avoid it, but sooner or later some vixens smile would slip a lovers knot on you when you wasn't looking. Or when you'd nodded off from too much ale.

"Put it 'way, Rat. Ain't no one getting stabbed today. 'Cept maybe the feller comin' down the road right now. Look lively, boys."

"Why're we starin' at this crossroads anyway, Darby, my man? Seems slim pickins'. Slim pickins', indeed."

"None of youse is a-ready for a better road Coal, *my man*." He put a dripping sneer into Coal's chosen rhetorical flourish. "Some of youse ain't never gonna be neither."

Darby boomed as he yanked his sword out of his scabbard. For a thief he had a voice that could carry for miles. Even his whispers carried too far, which might have accounted for his semi-retirement.

"Plus it's good for us. Less people a-means less guards and less patrols. Always go to where the a-patrols aren't, boy. It's the best way to stay alive."

"And poor," Rat muttered at the raindrops. They listened better anyway.

"You say something Rat?"

"Guards is where the best stuff is, Darby. You told me that."

That was a long while ago now, back when Darby was fresh back in town and the full glow of mystery still clung on his fancy fine cloak. Now his cloak was just as worn out as the rest of them, and his belly grumbled just as fiercely.

Darby shuffled his feet among the sodden leaves a little like a little kid fresh caught in a lie.

"Aye. I a-said that did I?" He cranked his head back up from where they lingered, looking at his toes. "And it's true. But it's also where all the a-pointy things are. Best to stick here until you learn the trade, boy. Now youse all get ready. He's a-coming up."

That was about when Finger lumbered up, the rain bouncing off of him like it didn't even exist. He clomped up close - too close - to Darby and stared down at him vacantly. You could almost see the ice-choked mountain wind drift wintery tendrils through the barren wasteland of his oversized and dull looking head. Very little lived in that giant head of his—perhaps a cockroach or two but not much else. He stared out at the world from that vast interior nothing with eyes that lingered somewhere between completely mystified and nearly asleep.

"What's happening?"

"Get ready Finger. Someone's coming."

"You want I should hit him with a branch?"

"Not just yet. Just get ready."

Which meant absolutely nothing to Finger. Getting ready to him meant staring at his hands and shuffling his feet as though he was trying to work out if there was something else he should be doing with them other than standing on them.

"Might want to get the branch, though. Just in case he needs bashing."

"Oh. Right."

Rat tracked the big idiot as he plodded over to a tree where he ripped off a low branch as though making a roasting stick for the fire. The branch was at least as big as Rat's own leg. He'd forgotten the fact that he'd done much the same thing only a few days ago and the branch he'd ripped off then now leaned abandoned against the fallen log he'd just gotten up from.

The rain kept coming. Through it, the road was just a hazy blue gap reflecting misty gray trees until both trees and road were little more than a darker shadowy smudge against a blotted gray sky. It was, he'd been told, a great spot to see prospective 'clients' coming. In the rain they tended to look like ghosts slowly resolving and sharpening as they approached. This one started out as a dark thickness through the droplets. Had Rat ever seen an elephant, he might have thought of it as he saw the figure approaching. As it was, he had almost no reference. It seemed to lurch as it walked and he felt each heavy footstep as it landed, shooting sad plodding shockwaves into his knees.

Through the constant spatter of the raindrops a low burble, like far distant thunder made from the hooves of great beasts, rumbled down at them. Rat felt the sound in his belly and through his chest as he skinned his dagger from its scabbard, shoving it up into the small of his back to hide it from view. Thunder arced down the mountainside, high and invisible above them contrasting to the burble as though to distinguish it for their benefit alone. It was as though the Gods themselves were reassuring him that this mumbling thing was not the mountain he seemed, but merely another man. Another 'Client' as Darby always put it.

But the God's thunder didn't thaw out his blood. It failed to reassure. Every step that pulled the form out of the droplets and spray of rain, every resonating footfall that marked his approach, every emerging gray detail of the thing's enormous form only increased the fear crawling up his body from the ash-gray mud. He glanced quickly to

Darby, but of course Darby was no where to be seen again. He'd vanished as he did when the clients approached. It was a trick he found himself wishing he'd learned.

Slowly, horribly, the things deep falling boulder voice made more sense. It's breath was like angry ghosts charging out of its still shrouded face, defiant of the sheets of rain that bounced off it's gray rocky hide.

"It is not my fault, Kyarka. There are none on the paths... No. I am trying." The thing appeared to be talking at his hands cupped in front of him as though trying to catch the water sliding off it's massive chest. "Don't say such things. I will be brave. I am not as wise as you. You must guide me."

The closer the thing got, the more Rat was uncertain whether he was hearing it's voice or feeling it bouncing off his own ribcage.

"Which way? To the right you say? To the humans? Why? What is there? Damn it, woman. You are like the stone you are made from. I liked your speech better when you were alive. Why right? Why humans?"

It was now within a mere ten feet and still hadn't glanced up from his cupped palms in front of him. If he knew they were there, he showed no sign of it. Instead, he slowly glanced from his palms straight past Finger at the road leading off to the right.

"I will go right, Kyarka. You were wise in life and I will trust your wisdom in death. Though I do not understand it. No. I am not worried about them. They are tiny."

For a moment it seemed like the great stone man would simply keep walking, thundering straight past them on his way as though they weren't even there. Rat hoped he would. But of course, that was the moment Darby reappeared with his own blade. Rat wasn't sure what he intended to do with it. He would need a ladder to get up to the man's neck and even then it would be like trying to hew through a tree with a butter knife made of wood.

"Trick or treat," Darby growled from behind him. Rat felt something warm flow down his leg.

The giant gray thing looked up from his hands straight into Rat's eyes. It was as though he saw a pebble in his path. Rat found himself shaking his head just a little trying to silently tell the huge thing that he wasn't the one who spoke.

"We played the trick," Darby growled to the man's enormous back. Even from the other side of him, he could see the giant gray things muscles ripple as he stood up a little more. "Now we get the treat. Hand over that pretty axe at your side. Nice and slow."

"These, Kyarka? Are you certain? If you find them acceptable you can have them, I suppose. No, darling. They will not lead me to you. If you think they are good enough, I will - though I would rather give you reward more fitting to your beauty...I did *so* think you were beautiful...I am *not* getting soft. My memory is as it was...Oh hush. You are...you always were too harsh. I was trying to be tender. I know it doesn't fit me but you are dead and I thought.... Yes. I know. Thinking is not what I am best for."

"That's enough chatter big man. Just give us the axe. And that other one on your back here. And whatever is in your purse..."

"Come, my good man. Come. It's just a little thing. Nothing to lose skin over. Just hand it over and be on your way. We don't want to hurt you."

"Shut up, Coal. If you know what's good for you." Rat hissed.

"Spit your balls out, Rat, my man. You're choking on them. There are five of us and one of him."

"Do I bash him yet, Boss?"

"Not yet, Finger. Just give him a chance to think about it a little."

The thing straightened a little bit more and took a deep breath, letting it out in a massive blue-white cloud which he somehow expanded into. Rat was more than a little disappointed to see he'd actually underestimated the thing's size - by quite a bit.

"I would like to play a trick," the thunder rumbled out of him with another breath.

"'At's not how it works big fella. We play the trick, see."

"It is a good trick," the big gray man continued.

"Oh. I like tricks. Can we see? Come on, Boss. It's no fun sitting here all day."

"No. Finger. We're not here for fun. This is business."

"Just the one. Come on."

The rain pounded on as Darby thought about it for a moment. The cloud of the rock-man's breath seemed to generate it's own storms. Rat felt any moment lightning would ripple out of it.

"If he puts down his weapons first. We can see the trick. How's that sound, big fella?"

"That is acceptable."

It didn't look any less menacing without the giant axe on its back, which it buried half the height of a man into the earth. The haft stuck out as tall as Rat. This made him feel - if possible - even worse.

"You." The thing pointed at Finger. "Come here."

A big, toothy grin ran the width of Finger's ruddy face. Without thinking for a second he'd dropped his branch to the ground and shuffled up towards the walking and talking boulder. Until he was standing in front of him, it was hard to see just how much smaller Finger was in comparison but now that he was it was like seeing an under-fed squire eyeing up a warhorse. Rat felt something ugly in his stomach threatening to come out. It was a good thing, he thought, there was so little of it.

The massive slabs of the things hands landed on Finger's own broad shoulders. Rat felt the ground shift under his feet but Finger simply stared up at the giant like he was staring into the eyes of the jolly old giftgiver himself. With one effortless move the giant spun Finger around like he was opening a door. When he was turned the Giant bent over like he was about to kiss Finger on the arse. Rat took a breath.

With one easy move the rock-man yanked Finger straight into the air by his ankles, dangling his fat stupid face over the ground. Water coursed down his face and onto the leaves but you could see he was smiling. Rat heard him giggle.

"Whee! This is great fun! Rat! You should try this! Do Rat next, big fella!"

"No. I think I will do the pretty one next."

And that was the last thing Finger said. Which was a shame. He was dumb and ate almost all of their food, but at least he died happy.

The rock man drove Fingers head straight into the hard packed ground. Rat heard the snap of his neck before he could even move but even had he been able to he wasn't sure which direction he'd go. Darby lunged hard with his blade but missed and charged straight forward towards them. Rat had to spin out of the way a little to not be run through. As he turned he heard a horrible ripping and popping noise like trees make in a fast frost. It was the sound the branch made when Finger ripped it off the tree. It was now the sound Finger made as his leg was torn from the rest of him.

Coal screamed and dashed forward with his own blade raised but Finger's leg swung through the air like a giant flail, clearing the space in front of the giant and sending the pretty boy flying off the path as though brushed casually aside by the hand of a slightly irritated god. That wasn't quite the end of the kid though. He tenderly but quickly pushed himself off the rock he'd landed on and scoured the nearby brush for the blade he flung mid flight. The giant man launched Finger's leg at his back as he searched. It spun in the air sending spirals of gore and blood in a crimson pinwheel.

Rat couldn't take any more. He leaned over and emptied what little lunch he had and then some onto the ground.

"Not fair, my man. Not fair."

Rat recovered in time to see Coal finally find his sword and turn towards the big man. He had to give him that much. Coal did have bravery. Not much sense though. He should be running. He should be a little more worried that the giant was now yanking his own axe back out of the ground.

The rock man didn't speak. He took two steps towards Coal who tried hard to mind what few lessons he'd been given. He tried to be patient and watch where the swing would come. The trouble was, as Rat now saw, he'd been trained by a moron. Coal feinted a quick dodge to his left, but the rock man had already factored it in and the blow came right over Coal's right shoulder and cleared out somewhere around his left hip.

"My m...," Coal started a taunt that he'd never finish and died awestruck that his feint hadn't work as he'd been told it would. He also died staring at the undersole of his own fancy boot. Somehow, in Rat's mind, that seemed rather fitting.

Scab was next. He was staring at the pieces of his sister's cousin and somehow it brewed up a bravery in him that he'd never had before.

"You'll have to pay for that, my friend. He and I were kin."

The rock man stared down again, and again with the regard one might give an ant.

Scab lunged badly but the thing walked into it anyway, just to prove that he could. The frail and ancient knife skittered against his hard skin as though Scab just tried to murder the wall of a chapel. There was a plaintive, barely audible snap as the blade broke off leaving Scab holding onto nothing but the pommel.

"Your fealty to your kin is admirable." The thing rumbled down at him.

"Thank you. He wasn't worth much, but kin is kin."

"I know how it is." The rock man nodded. "Turn around and I will make it quick. For your kin."

Scab sighed and turned just a little. Rat felt something tugging at him, but he was too stunned to look. He did when the great axe went straight through his friends neck as though it were made of nothing more runny lard. Scab's head sailed through the air and landed at his feet.

"Time to go, boy. There's fights you can win and fights you can't. Run!" Darby yanked at him. Of course he knew that. He'd known that from the beginning. He wondered why he'd been the only one. Darby was supposed to be the professional. Their fearless leader. He'd started the fight even though any moron with any sense should have known not to come up against this guy. And here he was about to run away when his whole crew had just been slaughtered. Where was the justice in any of it?

Oh right. He thought. They were bandits. Justice meant something else entirely to them.

Rat opened and closed his mouth a few times, wondering what would come out of it if anything. He wished his feet were flying like Darby's were, but they seemed rooted like the sodden trees surrounding him, and like them he could do little more than witness.

Darby's quick footfalls scattered wet leaves and squelched in the mud as he slipped and slid down the right fork of the crossroad. The sound he made was almost the same noise the huge axe made as it passed through Coal. He wondered, with not a little bit of stunned awe, if all weapons made the same noise when stuck into someone. He opened his mouth a few more times, as though to ask Darby's rapidly receding back about it, but no sound came out.

He turned back to the rock man. Scab's headless body crashed to his knees and slowly pitched forward. For a second he almost laughed, thinking what a mouthful of mud his friend was about to get, but then looked down at his feet and saw the man's mouth was shut tight and his eyes were closed - waiting for the blow that already came. Rat opened his mouth to say something else but rainwater got in so he closed it again. He did this two or three times. His teeth clicked on each other each time he shut it. No sound was coming out but he didn't know what sound would, when and if it ever did. It would be nice, he thought, to have some words in him when he died. Something he could say about it all. But nothing came to mind.

The rock man picked up the smaller axe he'd dropped on the ground what felt like an hour ago now. With one almost bored motion he threw it at Darby, who was still slipping and running down the eastern road. The axe spun over in the air with no arc - just a simple straight line as though drawn on a string attached to Darby's spine. The way time was moving it seemed to go slow - like it should have been an easy thing for Darby to just leap out of the way.

But he didn't.

He kept on running, his feet skating over the leaves, his legs pinwheeling very much like the blade catching up to him.

It could not have been thrown more perfectly. When it caught up with him it lodged right in the middle of his back, high up, very close to the neck and right between the shoulder blades. Darby didn't even explode in pain or exclaim in any way. His hands didn't reach for it. It was as though someone simply snuffed out his particular candle. He pitched forward as though planting his last step, missed, and landed on his face.

Rat looked around to see who was next. There was no one left. It was awfully quiet there in the rain with the rock man. His teeth clicked on each other a few times more as the man hoisted the giant axe on one massive shoulder and strode towards him just like a man with a question that he might just have the answer to.

"Where are humans?"

Rat opened his mouth a few more times but still nothing wanted to come out.

"Speak little man. My wife is impatient."

He had no idea what wife the giant was talking about but he guessed he'd rather not find out. And yet his voice still didn't want to work. He thought of sitting by his own wife's fire. She was a bad one, he knew. But it didn't matter anymore. She could bawl him out for the rest of forever - an eternity - and he would take it as the sweetest music in the world. She could boil the whole taverns socks and serve it to him as stew and he'd eat it with a smile. She could screw the tinker, the tailor and all the passing merchants and he resolved he would treat her like a queen the rest of his days. It no longer mattered what happened. He was - for the moment anyway - alive and anything from here until his dying day (which he hoped to prolong as long as possible) would be a gift.

He might even become a churchgoer. He didn't even know the local priests name, but if he managed to get out of this - he would learn it.

"Humans, little man. Where are they?"

"You want...I... I heard something." He found his voice. It sounded completely different to him now. And it was. He was a man reborn. A different man - dedicated to life, and liberty, and not dying terrifically horrible deaths. 'Rat', he thought, died with the others in this place. Garrat - his first name - was here now in his place. Garrat the Just, Garrat the Helpful, Garrat the Patient. Which wasn't like Garrat at all and never had been. Even as a child he'd been a grabby, muddy little runt with no patience for anyone but his own aching belly. But here he'd found it.

"What did you hear?"

"A convocation. To the east." He pointed down the way Darby tried to run. "Heroes are being called. To do great deeds. To quest."

"Heroes?"

"Like you. Great men, Just men. To do great things in the world. To the east. A convocation. You'll like it."

"Are you a bandit? My wife hates bandits."

Garrat - formerly Rat - said the first honest and truthful thing he'd said in what seemed like a very long memory and it came out of him sounding much more powerful than anything else he'd said in his life.

"Not anymore."

The mountain man glanced once more directly into his eyes but Garrat's fear was gone now. He knew he was safe. When the gray mountain man turned and stalked away the heavy thuds of his boots reverberated in his own ribcage and he let out a breath, consciously thankful that he still could. He watched as the man stopped at Darby. He saw the strange way Darby lurched and slumped back down as the axe was yanked out of his back. It wasn't horrible anymore. It just was. And that was good. He knew, in an instant, that he wouldn't even scrounge the bodies when the giant receded from view. He would simply gather his few things, not much to gather really, leave his own useless blade and head back home, anxious to plant the seeds of a little farm.

* * *

Cuhlyn trudged on through the wet. In a matter of a few miles he'd already forgotten about the bandits. He didn't know the road. Roads were things for men and horses. He preferred climbing and rock and high places. All roads felt low and ugly - places where you would never see an eagle and your mind only stretched to the next tree or turn. His wife died on the road.

"What did you learn from that experience?" He heard the little stone icon he'd made to honor his wife speak from the little pouch he wore at his neck.

"What experience is that, my love?"

"With the bandits. You dispatched them quickly."

"What bandits?" He wondered and then he looked down at his throwing axe, Little Tickle. A chunk of someone's spine and gristle was still stuck to it. He briefly wondered how it got there, but then remembered.

"What should I have learned, my love?"

"Not all bandits will be quite so inept, you big lummox. Pay attention. If you hope to live in this world you need to pay attention to your enemies. They are greater teachers than friends."

"They weren't my enemies, my love. They were simply brambles in the path. I would have left them had they let me."

"Well..." The little stone wolf whispered in words only he could hear. "Then that is another thing to learn. Never let a bandit live if you can help it. They are not as bad as the ones who set themselves against us, but they're still a scourge. Where bandits linger, evil grows."

"That is good sense. Should I have killed that last one?"

"No. He was a bandit no longer. You've done well. Now let us see about this Convocation he spoke of. It shows promise for your vengeance."

"Yes, my dear."

Nearby, a raven sitting on a low branch watched the big thing lumber past and caught the scent of blood clinging to him. Raven heard the thing speak but didn't know who he was speaking to, which was odd. People didn't generally talk when there was no one to talk to. But people were weird things. Particularly this one. It stank of rock, and death and purpose.

The raven watched his huge back dissolve into the driving rain. It caught the smell of fresh kill not far away, and launched itself from the branch it was sitting on to see what the man had done. It figured it would have a nice feast and then, when he'd had his fill, he'd head into the wind to follow the big man.

Something in his bird mind said this would be a good man to keep an eye on.

Blame it on Moonlight

Michael Walton

Blaine Starbuck was the luckiest man in the world. He didn't know it, of course. If he had known about his good fortune he might have come to rely on it, and there's nothing like being taken for granted to make Lady Luck seek out a new dance partner. Blaine was both completely ignorant of how good he had it and genuinely grateful for every good thing that came his way, so the Lady continued to blow on the dice of his life – but, being a capricious creature, she often did so in ways that made his life... interesting.

Blaine's latest stroke of luck had him standing outside what would soon be his former place of employment. Smoke rose from the delivery truck that he had been driving before it came to a halt with the aid of a telephone pole. "Honestly, Mr. Jepson," said Blaine to his soon-to-be former boss, "The brakes just went out!" He flashed a sheepish grin and added, "At least I kept it from running into the building."

Mr. Jepson clapped Blaine on the shoulder, which was no small feat considering how much Blaine towered over him. "I believe yah, kid," he said, "And insurance oughta cover it either way. But company policy says you can't have any accidents in a company vehicle, and that is definitely an accident. I'm sorry, Starbuck, but I gotta let yah go."

Blaine hung his head. "I understand, sir," he said. "I'll go clean out my locker." He shook Mr. Jepson's hand and slunk away on his latest walk of shame.

* * *

This was the third job that Blaine had lost in as many weeks. He always managed to find others, but the gaps in employment looked bad on his resume. They looked even worse on his bank statements, and this latest short check put him in real danger of not making rent. Since he was already on foot, his car having been repossessed two weeks ago, he figured he might as well start pounding the pavement right away. He squared his shoulders, hiked his chin up, and marched down the street in search of the perfect job... or, at least, a place that was hiring today.

While Blaine searched for "help wanted" signs, Lady Luck awaited her cue. It arrived in the form of a balding middle-aged man with a flustered look on his face and a cell phone stuck to his ear. The Lady blew a kiss that transmuted into a gust of wind that nudged the man into Blaine's path. The poor fellow's less than irresistible force rebounded from the nigh-immovable object that was Blaine Starbuck. The man had barely hit the ground when Blaine started apologizing.

"Oh, jeez, I'm so sorry, sir!" said Blaine. "Are you okay?"

"Yeah," the man replied as he looked up, "I'm fi... aye, aye, aye!" Blaine did his best to project "apologetic" and "non-threatening," but those attitudes are hard to pull off when you're six-foot-five and have shoulders in different zip codes. "Whoa, they grow 'em big where you're from, don't they?"

"That's what everybody says," Blaine replied. He reached down and hauled the man to his feet with as little apparent effort as if he'd been picking daisies. "You sure you're okay, sir? I'm really sorry, I should've been watching where I was going."

"No, no, my fault," the man said, "I shouldn't have been walking while I was on the phone. Aw, crap, my phone!" Blaine scooped the phone up and returned it to its owner. "Thank you, young man." He put the phone back to his ear to resume his previous conversation. "Joe? You still there? Dangit, lost him."

"Important call, eh, sir?" Blaine asked.

"You said it," the older gentleman answered. "One of my guys just called in sick, another is on vacation, and I fired the third this morning for sleeping on the job. And to top things off, my wife planned this big dinner with her family, and she'll skin me alive if I miss it!" The man sighed. "Ah, sorry about dumping my problems on you, young man. I suppose I'll have to cover the shift myself and deal with the wifely wrath in the morning. It's not like I can hire a replacement this afternoon."

Most people who saw Blaine would suppose that he was no great thinker, and they would be right, but he was smart enough to recognize the sudden knocking sound as opportunity.

"Sir," Blaine said eagerly, "It just so happens that I'm looking for a job, and I can start right away!" After a brief conversation and a handshake, Blaine walked away with his new boss Mr. Torrance, and Lady Luck congratulated herself on another job well done.

* * *

"And that door leads to the alley out back," Mr. Torrance said. "You'll only need to go out there to take out the trash at the end of the shift, or if you take a smoke break. Do you smoke?" Mr. Torrance surreptitiously pulled a pack of cigarettes from his pocket as he asked this; he hated smoking alone.

"No, sir," said Blaine, "Never touch the stuff."

Mr. Torrance hastily replaced his smokes. "Good for you, son, filthy habit." He indicated the desk and continued, "You've got monitors for the security cams there, but don't worry about checking the recorder tonight. Charlie spilled a drink in it when he fell asleep, and the guy won't be here to fix it until tomorrow." Mr. Torrance stepped back and gave his new security guard a quick inspection. "How's the uniform feel?"

Blaine shifted uncomfortably. "It's a little tight across the shoulders," he said.

"A parachute would be tight across those shoulders," Mr. Torrance replied. "Now, remember, my number's on the board with the numbers for fire and police. And if there's trouble, skip the heroics and call it in! You're not a cop, you're not even a rent-a-cop, you're just a pair of eyes and a keychain. Got it?"

"Got it, sir," said Blaine. "No worries, I got this."

"Yeah, I know," Mr. Torrance conceded, "I'm just not in any hurry to see my mother-in-law. Good night, Blaine." He turned to go, but he stopped after a few steps. "Oh, I almost forgot. There's been some mutt prowling that alley the last couple of nights. When you go out back, be sure you don't let it in the warehouse."

"Keep an eye on the place, call if there's trouble, don't let the dog in," Blaine recited. "I'm on it, sir!"

"Wish I could trade you," said Mr. Torrance. He strolled out the door, and then it was just Blaine and the merchandise.

The warehouse was quite spacious. A football field would have fit within its floor space, and that was just the ground floor. The second and third levels were equally long and broad with large open squares in their centers. One could see to the upper levels from the ground floor, and most of the ground floor was visible from upstairs. A freight elevator in the middle of the south wall obviated the need to haul heavy boxes up the stairs. Blaine spun around slowly to take in the labyrinth of stacked boxes. He spread his arms and shouted, "I am Working Man!" The bare concrete of the walls and floor had nothing to say to that, so they just returned the sentiment. Blaine swaggered over to his tiny desk and settled in for his shift.

It didn't take long for Blaine to discover how dull guarding a building can be. He made his rounds faithfully every hour, but that left him with several forty-minute blocks of time to fill. There was no computer and he didn't bring any cards, so solitaire was out. Sleeping wasn't an option, either; he knew that his predecessor had been fired for it, and Blaine was too conscientious for such dereliction in any case. Tomorrow night I bring a book, he thought. Blaine found himself going to high alert every time the building settled or a cat yowled a love song into the night. At this rate, he grumbled to himself, Six-thirty will take a long time to get here.

The hoped-for break in the routine arrived just after midnight. Blaine heard some kind of scuffle, accompanied by much snarling and whimpering and topped off with a clash of trashcans. It's that dog, Blaine supposed, I'll just go chase him off. Blaine got up and went to the door. He undid all three locks, removed the bar, and opened the door just enough to slide himself through sideways, flashlight first. He scanned back and forth until he saw the glow of yellow eyes reflecting the meager light spilling from the door. Blaine aimed his flashlight and clicked it on in hope that the sudden bright light would startle the animal into leaving. That expectation didn't survive his first sight of what was caught in the beam.

Blaine Starbuck was no expert on wildlife, but even he could clearly see that the creature before him was no stray dog. Its shaggy black pelt wasn't anything unusual, but its size was another matter. The beast was huge; its shoulders came almost up to Blaine's, and were just as broad. Its forelegs were much longer than its hind limbs, and it moved as if the creature itself wasn't sure if it was walking on all fours or dragging its knuckles. The head looked like some grotesque compromise between human and lupine features, but there was nothing ambiguous about the size and function of its teeth. The monster sported a set of choppers that looked like they could carve steaks off of a live buffalo. When the werewolf turned its gaze on the stunned security guard, its yellow eyes took on an attitude that suggested saying grace.

Blaine had excellent survival instincts. His body had already turned and started to run while his reason was still in denial about what it was seeing. The monster howled and bounded after him.

Blaine was halfway across the room when the werewolf hit the door. Blaine's conscious mind took the opportunity to tell his instincts that they should have locked and barred the door. His instincts replied that it was a little late for I-told-you-so, and they should shut up and keep running. Blaine heard the creature gaining on him, so he took a desperate ninety-degree turn into the maze of boxes. The beast tried to match Blaine's maneuver and spun out on the slick concrete. Blaine winced as he heard cardboard boxes crumpling on impact, and he winced again when he heard the beast clawing its way free of those boxes.

The collision bought the security guard time to get to the elevator, but he was already breathing hard. The werewolf, judging by the sound of its growls, was merely annoyed. Blaine dove into the elevator and gave silent thanks that it was already on the ground floor. The werewolf emerged from the stacks at a dead run and made a beeline for its prey. Blaine jabbed at the second floor button like a one-finger typist, but the door insisted on working at its own pace. The beast was a mere handful of seconds away when the door finally slid closed. There was a tremendous crash, and the door suddenly sported a dent that looked suspiciously like a werewolf's head. The elevator rose as if nothing out of the ordinary had happened, and the building stereo system launched into an instrumental of, "Looks Like We Made It."

Who turned that on? Blaine thought.

Lady Luck did her best to look innocent.

The elevator dinged and deposited Blaine on the second floor. He leaped out and looked around for someplace to hide or some kind of barrier to put between himself and the creature. The galloping steps that he heard on the stairs told him that there wasn't much time in which to think it over. Salvation came in the form of a steel cage marked "Secure Storage." His fingers fumbled for the correct key even as he ran. Blaine got the lock open and pulled the door wide even as the monster bore down on him. He spun inside the cage, pulled the door to and slammed the lock home a mere heartbeat before the werewolf hit the bars. The creature snarled and swiped at him, but Blaine backed up well out of its reach. The werewolf rattled the bars, but they proved too strong. Blaine used the apparent safety to catch his breath while the werewolf began to pace.

This would be a great time to call 911, thought Blaine. *Too bad my phone got mangled in the accident.*

Lady Luck grinned and ticked that item off of her list.

The creature growled as it paced back and forth in front of the cage. Its eyes roved as well, doubtless searching for a weakness in Blaine's little fortress. It didn't take long to find. The beast's face split in an evil grin, and it pointed upward with a massive paw. Blaine looked up and saw that the secure storage cage was open at the top. "Oh, snap," he said. The werewolf took a few experimental leaps, but it couldn't reach the top of the enclosure. The beast shrugged and walked away, and Blaine laughed. "Yeah! Take that, you dumb mutt!" He shouted. The creature ignored him and picked up one of the larger boxes. "Can't get me in here, Fido!" Blaine continued. The werewolf put the box down in a new location and went to get another. "Not so big and bad now, huh? In your face! In! Your! Faaa... oh, boy." Blaine had finally figured out that the werewolf was stacking boxes to form a staircase. It would soon be able to reach the top of the stacks, and from there it was just a hop, skip and jump over the bars.

Blaine's reason nudged his instincts and suggested that it was time to change drivers. Instinct agreed and handed over the wheel. Blaine quietly unlocked the cage door when the werewolf started to climb. The beast bounded to the top of the stacks and took two leisurely hops toward the cage. Blaine spun himself out the door the same way that he had come in when it made its final leap into the cage. The werewolf came down for a perfect four point landing at the exact moment that Blaine re-locked the door. The creature lunged, but Blaine was already out of reach. It tested the bars, found them just as stout from within as from without, and glared at young Starbuck. The monster turned and began stacking boxes against the cage wall. Whenever it found one marked "fragile," it deliberately slammed the box down before putting it in place. Blaine didn't let the feeling of that damage coming out of his paycheck prevent him from heading for the stairs.

Blaine started to go back down to the ground floor, but then he remembered that sporting goods were on three. Maybe there will be something there that I can use, he supposed. He jogged up the stairs and ran to check out the nearest stacks. Clothes, clothes, and more clothes, he thought as he perused the labels. Then he snapped his fingers and said aloud, "What am I thinking? Silverware is on one!" He trotted over to the elevator and moved to push the button, but the elevator dinged before he reached it. The door opened to reveal the werewolf's hulking form crouched within. The creature saw Blaine, and its face cracked open in a vicious feral smile.

Reason was still blinking in confusion when instinct shoved it aside and resumed the helm. Blaine backpedaled as fast as he could manage while the monster emitted a growling chuckle. The werewolf howled, bunched its legs and exploded out of the elevator in a tremendous leap. The world went into slow motion as Blaine slipped on a patch of floor that had been recently buffed to convenient slickness and fell flat on his back. The werewolf sailed past him, over the safety rail and out into empty space. The hunting cry segued into a whine of surprise that dopplered away with distance as gravity did its work. The wolf's call ended with a crash, and Blaine flinched at the sound of expensive consumer electronics breaking a werewolf's fall.

Blaine picked himself up and walked over to the rail. Looking down revealed the expected ruin of plasma screens as well as the broken body of the werewolf. Blaine pumped his arm and said, "Yes!" Then the beast groaned and rolled over. "No," the young man whined.

The creature sat up and took inventory of itself. Both legs and one arm were bent in places where they weren't supposed to bend, and the beast's torso had a scrunched-in look that suggested broken ribs. The werewolf reached over with one arm to set the other, bent double to set both legs, and then lay back to let the rest of its wounds sort themselves out. The creature glared up at Blaine during the entire operation with an expression that said, "You're going to pay for this, monkey boy."

Now what? Blaine thought. He could rush down to the first floor and start ripping open boxes of flatware in search of some actual silver, but he had no idea how fast werewolves healed. The beast could well be up and running the moment he stepped out of the elevator. It was no use going back to two, either. The trick that he'd used there was only going to work once. Reason and instinct consulted each other, shrugged, and admitted that they had nothing.

It was then that courage elbowed its way to the fore. If they were going to die anyway, it suggested, they might as well go out fighting! Reason and instinct started to object, but courage thrashed them both, bound them and gagged them, then stood at attention and awaited further orders.

Right, then, thought Blaine, *Fighting it is.*

He ran to the other end of the building where the sporting goods were and looked for anything that might be of use. He smiled as he saw some already open boxes spread out before him. It was almost as if someone had laid out exactly what he needed. Blaine dug into the first box and started building his werewolf trap.

The monster stepped out of the elevator ten minutes later with its teeth bared in threat. It turned its head back and forth to catch a glimpse or whiff of its prey. The werewolf stalked across the floor, nostrils flared, and growled in satisfaction as it approached the area where the sporting goods were stored. The scent of the prey was strong here, and there were few places to hide and no way to run. The hunt was almost over.

The beast was still twenty yards from the pile of opened boxes when Blaine stepped out of the stacks and shouted, "Hey, ugly! Over here!"

The guard ducked back between the boxes. The werewolf uttered its hunting call and followed him in. The creature saw Blaine run to the end of the row and turn a corner. The beast covered the distance in far less time than the man had and pushed off the boxes to make the turn... right into the volleyball nets strung across the aisle. The werewolf's momentum both wrapped the nets securely around its body and pulled several boxes down on top of it. The falling boxes dislodged a stack of dumbbells that rebounded from the monster's head and shoulders with a series of thuds.

Blaine then ran up behind the werewolf, having run a full circle through the next aisle over, and threw a small tarpaulin over its head. "Let's see how you like it, furball!" Blaine roared. He dove into the pile of boxes, grabbed a double-handful of werewolf haunch, and bit down with all his might. The beast's snarls of rage ended in a yelp of astonishment. The creature convulsed and threw Blaine end-over-end across the row.

Blaine saw a flash of light when his head hit the floor. Some part of him wondered if he could recover from being stunned before the werewolf was on him. Reason, instinct, and courage all shook their heads and said, "Nope."

Blaine had absorbed a lot of literary clichés concerning the approach of certain death, so his life dutifully flashed before his eyes. He was only twenty and had grown up sheltered, so it didn't take long.

When the replay reached the point where he was knocked for a loop after chomping down on his would-be killer, Blaine noticed that he was still alive. It was also awfully quiet. He opened one eye to check his surroundings. Finding no shaggy black beast waiting for him to wake up so he would see it coming, he opened the other eye. Blaine got up and looked across the row. The creature lay still beneath the tarp, and the guard was sure that it looked smaller. The cloth rose and fell in time with the sound of soft breathing. Blaine grabbed a tennis racket from one of the fallen boxes and carefully reached for a corner of the tarp. He yanked the cloth away and jumped back with the racket held samurai-style in front of him. What he saw was most definitely not the broken but recovering body of a shaggy black beast.

The girl had hair the same light-hungry black as the werewolf's. She was long-legged and muscled like an athlete. Her ivory skin was marred only by the bruises from where the dumbbells had struck and by an inflamed bite mark on her otherwise perfect buttocks. She was incredibly beautiful, and would still have been so if she had been wearing anything.

Then she opened her sapphire blue eyes, and that stunned Blaine even more thoroughly than had being knocked on his head. Lady Luck flashed Cupid a thumbs-up for the excellent shooting, then she slipped him a twenty and sent him on his way.

The girl sat up and looked over her body in amazement. "I'm free," she breathed. Then she turned her gaze on Blaine and favored him with the kind of feminine smile that makes any man feel like a hero.

"Uh," Blaine responded. The heroic feeling had not yet fought its way past the confusion. Chivalry took advantage of the lull to remind Blaine that the lady was underdressed for the occasion. He stripped off his uniform shirt and handed it to her.

"Thank you," she said. Blaine noticed a hint of an Eastern European accent. This intrigued him, but not enough to prevent him from turning away while she dressed. "Is good now," she announced when she was finished. Blaine turned back to face the girl and found her standing quite close. "My name is Ilsa," she said. "And you are called...?"

"Um, Blaine," the young man managed to say, "Blaine Starbuck." He was finding Ilsa's current state of dress distracting. That shirt wasn't quite large enough for him, and Ilsa stood almost shoulder height to Blaine. On her the shirt was barely long enough to be decent. "Uh, please don't take this wrong, but why am I not dead?"

"You break curse," Ilsa replied. "You bite me, and now I am free."

Blaine tried to wrap his head around that, but his brain needed a warm-up before it could bend that much. "Wait a sec... you mean, you stopped being a werewolf because I bit you?"

"Of course," said Ilsa, "If bite of werewolf can turn human into werewolf, then..."

"...The bite of a human turns a werewolf into a human," Blaine finished. "Okay, I guess that makes sense." Instinct, courage and chivalry decided that the girl was cute, so they should just go with it. Reason threw up its arms in disgust and retreated into Blaine's subconscious. "So, uh, what happens now?"

Ilsa smiled. "I go home," she said, "I help Mama with family business. No more hiding from people who can see signs of curse. That's how Papa die, you see," she said. Ilsa mimed firing a rifle, and Blaine nodded in sympathy. "But now I can help Mama with apartments."

"You own an apartment building?" Blaine asked.

"Oh, yes! Eight floors, and we have one floor to ourselves," Ilsa replied. "We clean, fix here and there... but Mama and I can't do big jobs like Papa did. It would be good to have man around the house again." She laid her hand over Blaine's heart and asked, "You are good with tools, yes?" His heart skipped at her touch, and Ilsa's smile grew even brighter when she felt it.

"I am good with tools, yes," Blaine answered, "My dad always said that I could fix anything." Ilsa's expression went from affectionate gratitude to rapturous adoration. Instinct, courage and chivalry agreed that this was good, and they strongly recommended that Blaine do whatever it took to get more of that.

"Then, how about this," she said, "You walk me home. You meet Mama, and we talk about you coming to help us."

"I don't know..." Blaine said.

"It is good job," Ilsa cajoled, "Pay is okay, and Mama and I cook for you. Best of all, rent is free. Besides," she added as she surveyed the damage around them, "I am thinking that you will not be keeping this job."

Reason leaned out of its corner and screamed that they should take the offer. Its fellow personality fragments seconded the motion.

Blaine looked upon the carnage and was forced to agree. "Okay," he said, "You've got a deal. But first we have to find you something else to wear, 'cause I'm going to need that shirt back. Then I have to make a phone call. After I'm officially fired, we can go meet Mama." Ilsa's smile brightened to supernova levels, then she grabbed Blaine by the neck and pulled him into a passionate kiss. Reason and chivalry protested that they hardly knew this girl, but Instinct flipped them the bird and stated that they were going to shut up and keep kissing.

* * *

"What the... how did... when... what happened here?" Mr. Torrance stammered. The look on his face as he examined the mess in his warehouse blasted clear through incredulity and went so far out the other side that it circumnavigated the emotional globe and came to rest back at incredulity.

"It's like I said over the phone, sir," said Blaine. "That stray you warned me about got in when I opened the door to check out a suspicious noise. Made a real mess while I was trying to catch her." Blaine put on his apology face; by now he had lots of practice. "I'm really sorry, Mr. Torrance."

Mr. Torrance shot Blaine a snide look. "Yeah, I'm getting that impression," he said. Mr. Torrance put his palm to his face and dragged it down over his chin. "Insurance will cover the damage, but there's only one thing that can cover this gross dereliction of duty. Starbuck... you're fired!" Blaine nodded and started to walk away, but Mr. Torrance stopped him. "Wait! You're rehired." At Blaine's look of amazement Mr. Torrance continued, "And now you're fired again. After a screw-up this big, this enormous, this utterly monumental, it wasn't enough to fire you once! Now get out of my sight!" Blaine slunk away and left Mr. Torrance in the wreckage of his once orderly warehouse.

Ilsa was waiting at the corner when Blaine walked away from the building. She greeted him with a bear hug and a slightly less combustible kiss. "All done?" she asked.

"Yepper, all done," he answered. "So, how far are we going?"

"Is not far," she said, "Only about three miles." She took hold of his arm, and they started walking.

"Three miles on foot isn't far?" said Blaine, "No wonder you've got such great legs." A question occurred to him, and courage opined that he might as well ask. "Say, when you were... you know... you looked pretty scary. How did anybody ever mistake you for a stray dog?"

"Oh, that is because I have no tags," Ilsa said dismissively. "That is why Papa bring us to the city. City people think anything that looks doggy is stray dog if it has no tags, and I never wore collar." Then she leaned in close and whispered, "But for you, I might," and gave him a light nip on the ear.

Reason glared at its compatriots, but chivalry pointed out that it was a little late for I-told-you-so, and they should shut up and keep walking.

Lady Luck looked on in satisfaction as the couple walked off into the night. Blaine Starbuck wouldn't need her attentions anymore; from now on he and his girl would make their own luck. She smiled as the young lovers twined their fingers together and allowed herself a moment to admire her handiwork. Then she closed her eyes, spun around three times, and danced off in a random direction to find some other poor schmuck to mess with.

Bedtime Stories

Lacey D. Sutton

In the frozen twilight of a midwinter eve, the weathered house loomed like something out of a Gothic novelist's wet dream. While it could not be described as a 'decaying hulk' or in any way a 'wretched dwelling', it still fulfilled its obligations with crooked shutters, wood-shingled walls as grey as the swirling smog, and far more broken filigree accents, snapped dowel-post railings, and decapitated finials than intact ones. It had once been the matchless empress of the neighborhood. Now a match might do it some good.

It was the kind of house children dared each other to enter, and then had mad-cap adventures to avoid the fallout of their prejudicial tomfoolery.

On this night, however, cheerful light shone through gaps in the slumping shutters in a manner most disappointing to both rash children and overly-excited writers. Loud music and laughter chased the light out into the empty street, caught up with it, did a little twirl and capered arm-in-arm over the cobblestones with drunken jollity. There was no life outside of the residence because it was all crammed inside.

"Happy Ho...!" a woman shrieked, the final syllables drowned out by the bangs of crackers and an off-key rendition of 'Jolly Holly.' The roundel was not half bad, but, because all the singers had begun concurrently and had not remained so for long, it was, in fact, entirely terrible.

If someone were to enter through the front door, push their way through the inebriated mob to the tiny door of the side stairwell, then climb up three flights of creaky stairs crammed into a space designed to give a cave dweller claustrophobia, they would emerge into the relative peace of an attic-nursery. The sounds of the revel downstairs were still audible, but pleasantly muffled.

An oil-lamp burned low on a bedside table. Unlike the rambunctious light downstairs, this more reserved illumination puddled on the adjacent bed and offered mere suggestions of what lay beyond the nimbus. Old-fashioned toys, their staring glass eyes and their gaping mouths full of chipped china teeth, were only hinted at by the weakest of reflections and the strongest of heebie-jeebies.

The slight susurrus and pop of the smoking wick added atmosphere to the tale being told to the two occupants of the bed.

"Ah, Phantasmagoria sapiens. Colloquially known as a 'ghost.' Note the transparency, but do not be fooled into believing that renders them harmless. These can be found practically anywhere it is dark except under the covers on your bed. So how do you stay safe from them?"

"Stay in our bed." The high pitched voices had the schoolroom's dull sing-song. Their atonal saw was the perfect counterpoint to the governess's nasal drone, like a two-string violin and a bagpipe playing a funerary dirge.

"Correct. Because waiting for children who get out of their beds at night…." Ms. Small turned the page, the thin fingers of her right hand stroking the rough page as the uncalloused pads of her left caressed the embossed leather of the cover. This was her favorite story, and she savored the moment as a barbarian warlord would the sight of an unfortified village. This tale was her chief weapon in the battle to make naughty children behave.

"Waiting for those unlucky children, is Bedkeeper Betty."

The governess tilted the large book so that the boy and girl snuggled under the thick down comforter could see the page. Filling the page was a black and white woodcut illustration, comprised more of grisly passion than artistic skill. Jagged, hewn lines slashed out an image of a poster bed occupied by a child with stringy black hair and skeletal features. Her wide, inky eyes drew viewers into a staring contest, to the extent that the peripheral detail of the prone form of the bed's original unlucky occupant on the floor might almost go unnoticed.

There were no words on the page, but Ms. Small didn't need any prompting. Didn't they say a picture was worth a thousand words? Besides, she liked to tailor the tales to her audience.

"Once upon a time, there was a little girl named Betty. She was spoiled and contrary, and the thing she was most contrary about was staying in bed her at night. The minute her governess left, she would get out of bed and dance around her room and play with her toys and make mischief until she fell asleep where she was playing. Every morning she would wake up, cranky, and crabby, and sore, but no matter what her poor, hardworking governess said, she just wouldn't stay in her own bed.

"Well one night Betty was dancing around her room, and happened to look out the window. The moon was so beautiful, and the night was so clear, that she climbed out her window, and even though it was cold, decided to climb down from her roof to dance in the garden.

"She soon got very, very cold. She tried her front door, but it was locked. She tried to climb back onto the roof, but her fingers and feet were too cold to let her climb. Finally she fell asleep underneath a tree in the garden...."

The governess glanced over her wire-rimmed glasses to judge the effect so far on her audience. Pleased at the rapt attention, she pushed the glasses back up her nose with one finger and continued.

"AND SHE DIED! Not only that, but poor Betty's hands and feet froze right off." Her bony digit tapped the illustration, and the children could indeed see that the bed had no tell-tale bumps where feet might be expected, and that the emaciated arms ended in dark stumps.

"Cor!" little Master Humphrey said appreciatively, but snapped his lips shut when Ms. Small gave him The Look.

"She died for want of a nice, warm bed. Now she spends every night hunting for one. She sits outside of the bedroom windows of little children. If you leave your bed -- for *any* reason – Betty will slip in through the window and take your place. And when you come back...." After a significant pause, Ms. Small drew her finger across her throat, making a noise that was somewhere between a choke and someone squishing a toad.

There were a few beats of silence as those in the room digested this revelation. Ms. Small sat back with a smile and snapped The Book shut. It looked as if her work here was done – just in time for her to join the party below stairs.

Ms. Small had been the governess for many families over the years, and her favorite part of the day was when she tucked the children into bed and then didn't have to be a governess again until morning. Most children became restless, however, when bedtime came early enough to squeeze in a few chapters of her novel before she had to blow out her own lamp, or to join the other servants for a nightcap below stairs. Her position left her straddling the domestic world, but Ms. Small was not too top-lofty for a shared bottle of Elephant's Thud, or a dip into the holiday punch bowl. She hoped in that none of the other servants in this new household were too backward to let her.

This was her first night in the Thacker house. The last governess had departed two weeks before when she had married, of all scandalous things. The kind of governess who had the time to be courted on the job was obviously a lay-about – certainly Ms. Small had always been too busy to spend time on such things! – and so these children needed a firm hand right from the start. The family was just lucky that she was available to start the night of a holiday.

Not that she had anywhere else to be. Ms. Small had loved her last position, but even she had to admit that a catatonic child no longer needed a governess.

However, it was with pride that she could say that Little Miss Caroline had perfected staying in her bed when Ms. Small and The Book had finished with her.

Ms. Small picked up The Book up and began to stand. Then to her dismay there came from the bed the single most dreaded sound in the governess's world – the prelude to A Question.

"Miss… why does Betty kill the children? She just looks cold. Wouldn't it be warmer to share the bed?" Little Miss Violetta's eyes were enormous pools of crystal blue. And far too innocent for a seven-year-old at bedtime. This was a girl who had spent her lifetime waging the Battle of Sleep, and hence would be canny despite her youth.

"Oh yes," Master Humphrey agreed. "Bed is awways warmer wif sister in it." His little orange curls bounced with his enthusiastic nods, as if he never in his life had kicked or pinched his sister fighting over the precious middle-of-the-bed territory. He snuggled into Violetta, and she hugged him back – detente declared over this new threat to their sovereignty.

"Betty kills the children because she's a horrible, greedy little girl, and because they were foolish enough to get out of bed," Miss Small snapped. "There are more things out there that come after silly little children." The Book flopped back open to another grim scene.

This showed a little boy dangling his foot out of bed, clearly in the act of sneaking out as the mischievous smirk on his face attested. Pity for him that he didn't see the large, thick-fingered and fur-covered hand reaching for his ankle from beneath the bed. The stark black-and-white of the woodcut was not the best for showing detail, but the glint of fangs under the bed skirt was clear enough.

"Diablo sublectulus." The words left Ms. Small's lip with sibilant satisfaction. This was a threat the children couldn't pretend to empathize with! "The Bogeyman. There is one under every child's bed, my dears. So what should you never, ever, do at night?"

"On most nights, we shouldn't get out of bed, Miss. But this night, Mr. Constantinople is downstairs at the party. Daddy invited him. He said that as long as Mr. Constantinople stays behind a door, Daddy would have Jenners or one of the maids slip him a beer from time to time."

Ms. Small just blinked at the pert little miss in bed. What kind of child knew her Bogeyman's name? There was just the smallest crack in Violetta's mask of innocence. It hinted at a smirk much like the one sported by the little boy in the picture.

For the very first time in a long history of traumatizing children into obedience, Ms. Small felt her faith in The Book wobble. What had that trollop of a former governess been teaching these children? They had gotten…ideas. Children weren't supposed to be getting ideas under a governess's tutelage! They were supposed to be learning!

With a sound like the earth moving, she flipped to the next page.

This showed a girl with bouncing ringlets, holding a lit candle to sneak down an otherwise black staircase. The candle's light glinted off a pair of protuberant eyes visible through a gap in the riser, and on the stair that the little girl was about to put her foot onto were the marks of what might be nail-scratches from prior victims dragged through the gap and into the darkness behind.

Ha! Ms. Small thought, but before she could launch into her story of horror, she saw Master Humphrey shaking his little head.

"Poor Mr. Ickie. Our wast gowwerness caught him peeking up her skirts, and beat him to deaff wif a poker."

With another crack, The Book was flipped to a new woodcut.

The stark black lines delineated a fur-covered creature with the head of a wolf and the haunches of a man, blood dripping from its maw and the severed limbs of its hopefully deceased prey held club-like in each thick-fingered paw. Judging by the dimensions of the limbs, the implication was clear that these were the remains of a child.

"Homo lupus," Ms. Small said with a hairline crack in her voice. "They hunt at night, and their favorite prey are little children, because they're just so delicious." Ms. Small was practically salivating herself at the idea. Her supper had been postponed by these impish children. Although the smells from the revels on the first story could not penetrate all the floors between, the ideas of those smells did, and they hard-boiled Ms. Small's determination to end this battle now.

"If one of them catches you out of bed at night, he will rip you apart and feast on your soft guts. He will save your eyeballs for last so that you may see him eat every last bit of you. Now! What do you say to that?!"

The occupants of the bed were silent for a moment, staring at the monochromatic horror.

The quiet was too good to be true. Violetta broke it with a determined chirp, "I would take a ball with me and see if he wants to play fetch."

The Governess sat in silence for a moment, regarding her charge through narrowed eyes. "And you would die," she growled.

"But Miss! Billy Cobwell is a werewolf, and he wuvs to pway ball." Humphrey's lower lip was definitely sticking out at a mutinous angle.

It was like getting a canon-ball to the gut. Miss Small was floundering. These were the most horrible monsters imaginable, and never before had one of her charges suggested playing with one. The Book was running out of pages. With trembling fingers, she pushed against the bridge of her glasses and then eased to the next page.

"Trollus trollus," she got out, then hesitated at looked at the bed.

Sharp blue eyes like gimlets stared back at her.

"Mummy asked Mr. Pyrite if he wanted some molten sulfur when he came over to dinner the other night, and that seemed to do the trick." There was no longer any pretense in the girl's face. This was open war. There would be no prisoners.

With numb fingertips, Ms. Small turned to a new page at random. She no longer cared what story she landed on, and yet could not bring herself to admit defeat.

Violetta's eyes darted down to the page…and all color drained from the child's rosy cheeks. Humphrey leaned around his sister for a better look, then his own face paled, freckles showing on his pallid skin like shrapnel wounds. Both of the children's stares flicked up to wander around Ms. Small's features, then returned to the page.

Violetta's elbow nudged Humphrey and then she lay back down on her pillow and dragged the comforter up to her chin. Her brother followed her example and went so far as to close his eyes.

"Goodnight, Miss," Violetta's voice was flat and then she too shut her eyes.

"Goodnight, Miss," Master Humphrey echoed, then added some soft snores for good measure.

Ms. Small blinked. She glanced down to see the "About the Author" page that her careless fingers had revealed. Her vanity had been wounded at the harshness of the portrait when it had been chiseled into the soft wood, but she knew that Mr. Kellan had done his best for the meager sum she had been able to pay him.

With the glint of a victory pulled from the ashes in her eye, Ms. Small snapped The Book shut. "Goodnight, children," she said primly as she rose, holding back the urge to crow. One victorious night would make the battle tomorrow that much easier. Soon her reign over the nursery would be absolute and uncontested! Her bony fingers turned the key on the oil lamp to snuff the wick, and she picked her way across the toy-strewn floor to the narrow door.

She returned to her room long enough to place The Book with loving care on the bedside table, and to let down her hair. The long, midnight waterfall was her best feature. Not that she had any intention of attracting masculine attention, but there no fault in putting her best foot forward, was there?

Very nearly dancing down the back stairs, Ms. Small emerged on the ground floor into a press of bodies and a volume of discourse that was almost a physical guest in its own right. Slipping towards the buffet, Ms. Small heaped a dainty plate with not-so-dainty cuts of rare meat, dripping with juices. Dealing with those children had left her with the urge to bite something and watch it bleed.

She held the china with as much delicacy as the weight allowed and added a bread roll to sop up every last drop. The glass of something straw-colored and frothy from a passing tray that she snagged from a passing tray was the perfect cap to her triumph. With a pleased smirk, she sought out a place with fewer celebrants.

She found her escape through a doorway into a deserted corridor. Ms. Small put her plate down on a small credenza and took a deep sip from her glass. The contents were revealed as a light lager, and she let the bitterness wash away the memory of her near-defeat in the nursery. Tomorrow was another day, another fight, but for tonight she had won.

Ms. Small glanced around to make sure she was alone, and then raised her glass to salute that victory.

"Why...Ms. Small, is it?" came very deep voice from behind her. It was the kind of voice that sent shivers up the spine because it was all too often followed by the forceful removal of that structure. It held reverberations of all that mankind feared in the dark, with extra sharp bits.

"Y...yes?" Ms. Small did not turn around. After all, she had just looked; there had been no one there.

"A pleasure to meet to you, ma'am. Always happy when I have the opportunity to speak to a fellow Child Bedtime Enforcement Professional. Allow me to introduce myself. I am Mr. Constantinople. I believe the children told you about me?"

The name rang distant bells, which swelled into alarm claxons.

"The bogeyman?" The governess gulped a dry throat. Then she raised her glass to her lips and gulped a very wet mouthful.

"That would be the one," Mr. Constantinople chuckled. "Diablo sublectulus, I believe you termed me – the devil under the bed. Very amusing, if not quite accurate. You see, we bogeymen are not confined to beneath the bed – we also inhabit closets, behind doors... anywhere that is sufficiently dark and...private. But we can emerge from our refuges, as needed."

There was a sensation of pressure on Ms. Small's back – not a physical pressure, but that psychic awareness when there is suddenly something very large immediately behind you. The impression amounted to a push, but Ms. Small did not yield and run. There was nowhere to run to, after all. She knew that better than anyone else.

"You were upstairs when I was reading to the children?" she asked the wallpaper at the far end of the hall. The mirror to her left pulled at her eyes as much as the force behind her pushed, but she did not cave to that either. Some things were not meant to be seen. Others would lurk eternally in the dark of the eyelids, hijacking passing thoughts and dragging them back when the sight first struck.

"Oh yes. I take my duties very, very seriously, you see. I know the children said that I had been invited down to the party, and that is the truth. But I could never leave before they were all tucked in, safe and sound. But once they fall asleep, I do appreciate the opportunity to get out and stretch my legs."

The awareness of something large magnified as Mr. Constantinople followed through on his words, until Ms. Small had to stifle the urge to scream.

Before she could succumb, the bogey gave a happy grunt, and the sensation subsided from Mt. Everest to simply looming. Then there came the rustle of paper – not of a book but of a few loose sheets being shaken and straightened as the holder prepared to be a reader.

"I might have something of interest to you. I received the most fascinating letter from an old acquaintance of mine – a fellow CBEP. I had inquired as to his health after he missed our weekly canasta game for the second time in a row. The circumstances surrounding his absence are most unusual. I say, Ms. Small, do you mind if I move a smidge more into the light. My eyes aren't what they once were."

"Be...be my guest."

"Very gracious of you," Mr. Constantinople said as looming became incipient crushing. "Now let's see. Poor Bernie writes that he is having the most miserable time of it. He is in perfect health, but unfortunately the child under whose bed he resides – Ms. Caroline Happlepenny – is in a very sad state indeed. She is bed-bound – oh joy! – but unfortunately instead of being unconscious so that he can slip out and keep to his nocturnal schedule, the little darling's eyes are perpetually open and she lets out the most alarming screams at the slightest noise. He is writing the head office for a re-assignment, but holds out little hope because, as you know, every child needs a CBEP. If he can't be reassigned, he will have to accompany Miss Caroline to the mental ward, and those linoleum floors are a beast on a poor bogeyman's back.

"I wouldn't have bothered you with this, of course – especially during a party – but Bernie asked specifically to be remembered to you, should our paths cross. As now, happily, they have."

There was the sound of the letter being folded, and then silence stretched the length of the little hallway before returning rather sheepishly when it found it was still wanted.

Finally Ms. Small dismissed it. "I am not afraid of you. You are a bogeyman for little children. You can do nothing to me."

"Oh, my heavens, Ms. Small. Perish the thought! But again, I must correct you on one thing. Bogeymen are not just for little children. We are for those who believe in us, those who not only spread our tales but who take us into the darkness inside their hearts. And you have made a very fine home for us indeed. Almost an honorary bogeyman, you are.

And because of that, I am not here to hurt you. You see, for my sins, I just happen to be a member of the CBEP council. I am here to extend to you a job offer."

Ms. Small laughed, most of her fear vanishing before the ridiculousness of this conversation. "As a bogeyman? Pull the other one, it's got bells on!"

"Well, no," Mr. Constantinople confessed. "It is the sad state of these otherwise progressive times that my occupation remains barred to females. But there is a similar position, tailored exclusively to females. I don't suppose you have heard of the Bedroom Hag?"

Ms. Small's thoughts flicked to The Book, and the illustration in it of a black-clad, black-haired woman who was nearly part of the nursery shadows, watching, waiting, for the child in the bed to move. The hag was skin stretched over bone, sharp-featured and sharp-toothed. When Ms. Small had first seen the picture she had been impressed… then had flipped to the "About the Author" page to confirm a suspicion. Of all the cheek – Mr. Kellan had used her own face as his model!

Had that been a coincidence? Or had the old man's milky eyes seen something beneath the surface?

"I…I decline your kind offer, Mr. Constantinople." Ms. Small's voice had a pleading quality to it. Her current life might be limiting, but she could at least stop being a governess when the children were in bed. Day or night, the Bedroom Hag could never be anything but the monster in the corner of the nursery.

"It isn't really an offer you can refuse, Ms. Small," Mr. Constantinople said softly. And then the avalanche descended.

A short time later a large hairy hand took up the abandoned plate and the glass of lager, and retreated back to his refuge behind the door.

Katie the maid was kind enough to drop off a fresh glass of champagne just before midnight, when the celebrants in the other room shot off their poppers. The sound of the party was died away as celebrants spilled in little rivulets out of the house, to tread the snowy streets back to their own homes. Finally, in the cold hours before dawn, the last of the lights were snuffed out one by one and tranquility returned to the house from wherever it had been taking a smoke.

In the peaceful silence of a sleeping house, Mr. Constantinople tipped back the last drop and gently set down the fluted glass. He stretched one last time, and then crept through the empty rooms to the side-stairs.

He paused for a moment in the vacated governess's room to pick up The Book. From under the bed he had been unable to see the pages. As he flipped through it now he was unimpressed. Ms. Small had done her research but the execution was flawed. Not by the artistry – which was as efficiently workman-like as a hammer to the face – but by the author's intent.

Terrifying children into remaining safely indoors all night was a thing of delicacy, constructed of shadows and weird noises. This book was a hurricane in a profession that merely called for a puff of breath where none was expected. Mr. Constantinople tucked it under his arm. It went against the grain to burn books, but tomorrow night he just might make an exception.

He was a little sorry for poor Caroline Happlepenny for being saddled again with her own personal nightmare. But since a bedroom hag was assigned to a bedroom and not a child, their newest CBEP would be forced to stay behind in the empty nursery when the girl was taken to the asylum. And surely some poor bogart at the hospital could be counted on to do double-duty. It wasn't like the girl was going anywhere. Best of all, now Bernie could find a household with nice active children to give the fright to, and when they all settled into a comfortable routine he could make it out to game nights once more. So it would all come right in the end.

As for his own work...Violetta and Master Humphrey might have been given more ideas than sense by their last governess, but they hadn't deserved Ms. Small. Even if they bordered on the overly familiar at times, they knew enough to respect him. It wasn't abject terror that a hardworking bogey really wanted. Respect for the arrangement was better than a child too afraid to grope for the goes-under any day. It did mean fewer nighttime accidents dripping through the mattress.

Giving a friendly wave to Betty where she sat swinging her leg stumps on the window-ledge, Mr. Constantinople slipped into his space under the bed. It was a tight squeeze, but it was home. As he relaxed, the sounds of the settling old house filtered in.

Those who thought it looked like a house for monsters were only partially correct. It was a house *run* by monsters, as most were, but this one was made happier by the knowing cooperation of its inhabitants. Pleased to have been able to once more do his part, Mr. Constantinople joined the rest of the house in sleep.

Final

D.R. Perry

The covers, white and cold much like the snow,
Her hands above them reaching up to mine;
The time's not right, and so no tears will flow.

I said I loved her. Mama said, "I know,
I love you too," then dozed, closed hazel eyes
With eyelids white and cold much like the snow.

She woke, her thoughts leaves, fallen and windblown.
"Oh? Who are you?" She didn't recognize
My face or me; I will let no tears flow.

I smiled and stood, she gave me leave to go
(She sang "que sera sera" like goodbye)
In that room white and cold much like the snow.

And at the airport, time and I fly home.
That breath she knew me, a bright stolen prize;
Heart's souvenir I hold so tears won't flow.

In black and bundled, standing in the cold
I shovel earth. The Rabbi's eyes are wise.
She's gone, the grey cold sky produces snow.
Yes; now it's time, and so the tears do flow.

THE LONGEST NIGHT WATCH

Acknowledgements

Thank you

The editor, Lacey D. Sutton, would like to thank all of the authors who contributed their stories and poems gratis to this good cause. Many of them took the trouble to comment on the others stories, including hers, and saved her time during editing. Melissa Oenning and Linda and Tom Stumbaugh: thank you as well for helping hammer "Bedtime Stories" into something to be proud of.

Andrew Barber would like to thank Gen Wren, for being awesome and his biggest fan.

Janet Gershen-Siegel wants to thank Jay, who keeps her grounded as they reach for the stars.

D.R. Perry extends special thanks to Estelle, James and SKY.

R.R. Virdi would like to thank everyone who buys/reads this book. Thank you for taking a look at our works and helping a good cause. You're wonderful people.

The Night Watchmen would also like to thank Chelo Felice Biggerstaff, whose brainchild this anthology was and who was kind enough to pass it along when circumstances prevented her from taking it to completion.

We look forward to seeing you again next year.